Let's Pretend

LINDSAY ROCHESTER

Cover: Melody Jefferies

Editing: Natalie Gray

Paperback: 979-8-9881004-8-5

E-book: 979-8-9881004-9-2

Library of Congress Control Number: 2025916742

Published in Ellenboro, NC

Addison Pierce Publishing

LindsayRochester.com

For Fran

My mother-in-love

And the strongest person I know

You made it! And I'm so very thankful

1

ALEXANDER

"Alexander! Alexander, over here!" I look toward the man calling to me, my biggest Hollywood smile on my face. This isn't my favorite part of my life, but it's necessary, and I don't usually mind it. Still, my smile isn't one hundred percent genuine.

"What can you tell us about the rumors we're hearing that you proposed?"

Well, this is new. I guess I have my agent to thank for this. Or my girlfriend's agent. Either way, there isn't one ounce of truth to them; our relationship isn't even real. Our agents put our relationship together to help create interest and drive our careers even further. I only agreed because I hoped it would help with women throwing themselves at me. It hasn't. And also, because Grey Blankenship is a genuinely great person, and I thought ... who better to be forced to hang around with?

She's become one of my closest friends, so, ultimately, it's worked out. We have a lot of fun. But romantic interest? No. She's actually seeing someone from her hometown. Nearly got caught snogging him behind the Ferris wheel at their county fair. I keep telling her she needs to try harder to be discreet. And as for me? She just isn't my type. While I wouldn't say straightlaced and mild is my type, Grey falls on the far other side of the spectrum. I think I'd prefer a woman somewhere in the middle.

But for friendship, Grey is great.

"We'll never tell." She comes up and grabs my arm, answering the reporter. She smiles effortlessly, completely in her element.

We make our way down the red carpet together until Grey answers the call of her adoring fans. I walk toward the shadows. I've done enough obligatory posing, smiling, and waving, so I opt to try to fade into the background. It isn't long, however, until I'm approached by my costar, Crescent Wright. I have grown increasingly tired of her and her efforts to seduce me. I will never do another movie with her.

Now I regret my choice to leave Grey's side.

I generally like my movie premieres, as long as I can get away from the chaos of the red carpet as quickly as possible, but

Crescent made me dread this one.

"I can't believe we're finally here. I'm so excited," Crescent says, threading her arm through mine.

Not wishing to make a scene, I let her stand there, clinging to me. "Yes. The film is going to be lovely."

"Yes. The film is going to be lovely," she parrots back at me in a truly terrible imitation of my English accent. It was one of the many ways she annoyed me during filming *The Mark of Everlore* and the entire press junket. She laughs as if she were the most charming and clever girl to ever grace the earth. "It is, isn't it? You know what scene I can't wait to see on the big screen?"

Our kiss. She can't wait to see our kiss. I feel my stomach turn and have to school my features in order not to give the cameras a truly terrible photo for the world to dissect. That scene was, by far, the hardest scene I've ever had to film, and not because we filmed it in a tiny, damp cave.

When I don't answer, she continues. "Our kiss. I think the magic and chemistry will jump off the screen. Don't you?"

I'm hoping I'm a good enough actor that my *discomfort* doesn't jump off the screen. I'm certainly tapping into my acting skills right now with dozens of cameras pointed in our direction.

As it turns out, Crescent is right. Our kiss is captivating. At least, that's what I hear—and what I can attest to based on the first three seconds I saw before training my eyes on the bottom-left corner of the screen. I take a bite of shrimp and immediately regret it. Seafood and the memory of that scene aren't an ideal combination.

The afterparty is something I would legitimately enjoy, but yet again, Crescent is there to do what Crescent does. She's glued herself to my side. I look down to where she stands, pressed against me, and take a subtle step away. She is absorbed in conversation, so I assume she won't notice. But she does and steps close once more. Why do I have to be so nice? Strike that. I'm not really nice to her anymore. The better question is, why do I not tell her once and for all how obnoxious she is and that I want her to stay away from me?

Because my mother would roll over in her grave, that's why.

"I'm afraid I need to steal this guy," Grey says as she walks up and pulls me from Crescent's side, not giving her a chance to respond.

"Where have you been?" I complain as we head toward the drinks.

"I was on the phone with Conner." She smiles at the mention of her high school sweetheart. "And don't fuss at me; you could have left Crescent at any point."

I sigh. "I know. I can usually get away with subtle hints, or maneuvers to get my message across, but with her ... I don't know. Nothing ever works, and at this point, I just have to make it to the end of the party, and I'll never need to see her again."

"You are too nice."

"You would have made her cry on several occasions by now."

"Yes. And I would not still be dealing with"—she waves her hand in Crescent's general direction—"all of that."

"Yeah, yeah, o' wise one."

"Now kiss my cheek and tell me how beautiful I am." Grey bats her eyelashes at me and grins.

"I don't think I will."

"See, there's the attitude you need with her." She pats my shoulder. "Come on, my makeup artist, Misty, brought her best friend as her plus one, and I want to introduce you."

"What? No. You're my *girlfriend*."

"It won't hurt for you to meet her. Misty is great, so I'm sure her best friend is too."

I sigh and go with Grey. Maybe this is a good thing. I've known for a while that I don't want to date anyone within Hollywood. I love the work, but I don't love the life, and generally that's not how people here feel. It could be good to meet a "normal person" who is Hollywood-adjacent.

Unfortunately, that's not how this meeting goes. Misty's friend, Nev, is trying to break into Hollywood. She's obviously romanced by my connections and what she assumes is in my bank account. Not happening, Nev. Gee, thanks, Grey.

2

IVy

"Anizey!" The name I've been called by my niece and nephew since my niece began to talk and blended the words aunt and Ivy makes me smile. "Mama said if you don't come down for breakfast, she's gonna feed your portion to Minerva and then come lay on top of you until you can't stand it anymore." My niece Juniper's voice comes through the door as it does every morning, with various threats that my sister never makes good on.

I joined them on my first morning here, and feeling like an intruder in their morning routines, I decided to leave them be at breakfast. I assume the dog's been eating well in the mornings since I moved in.

Maybe moved in isn't correct. I'm only here temporarily.

Until recently, I lived above the restaurant I own. I grew *Bowl* from a small food truck to a prime location on Main Street. We may live in a small town, but people need to eat, and they seem to love to eat my food. Everything on the menu comes in a bowl. We specialize in breakfast bowls, but later in the day we also offer soups, hearty salads and other bowl-able non-breakfast fare. Oh, and ice cream with a topping's menu containing almost anything anyone has ever dreamed of putting on their dessert and then some.

But it burned down. I mean not literally; the bricks are fine. The building still stands, but everything else is gone. The manager I hired and trusted—much like I imagine a parent handing over their child to a babysitter—left one afternoon without double-checking everything, and that evening I received a phone call that my life as I knew it was over. At least for the time being.

Thank God I was gone for the weekend, visiting my college roommate in Virginia. At least I'm still alive, even if my business is temporarily gone.

I turn onto my side, pulling the covers up to my neck, just as I like them. I have a minute of quiet before a banging on my door signals my niece's return.

"Mama says you're thirty years old. You need to put on your big girl pants and come downstairs. You can't rot in that room."

I jump up and fling the door open, startling Juniper. "Why can't your mother come and threaten me herself?" I ask, feigning anger.

"She's busy cooking."

"Nah. I think she's just too scared," I joke, and my niece just stares up at me. "Fine. I'm gonna go to the bathroom. I'll be right down."

Juniper eyes me suspiciously. "Will you? Because I don't want to have to come back up here."

"Yes, sassy pants, I will. I'd hate for your poor nine-year-old legs to have to drag you back up here."

"Thank you," Juniper says with a satisfied smile before heading to the stairs.

I trudge into the bathroom, already knowing what I'll see. My paper-white skin will be dull and lifeless—apart from the extra freckles the sun has drawn on my skin—and my golden-brown curls will resemble a tumbleweed. At least I assume tumbleweeds are brown. I've never seen one in real life.

I don't turn on the light because I know if I did, I would want to try to fix things. The night-light will have to do. I don't have five minutes, much less the surely necessary half-hour, before my sister sends Juniper back up here.

I quickly use the bathroom and brush my teeth before heading downstairs.

"Well, look who it is, and before eleven a.m.," Val, my now

morning-person younger sister, says as she drops butter into a pot on the stove. I remember the days when I had to wake her and get her ready for school. Back then, her night-owl self made everything difficult in the mornings. People can change.

"I've been consistently sleeping in for the first time in the last decade. I'll not let you beat me up about it."

"Sleeping in is one thing. You've been sulking and you know it. It's time to do something."

"Like a puzzle?"

"Like anything; I don't care."

"I've not been sulking. You know that's not my personality. I get up once y'all leave. I felt like I was in the way that first morning."

"You're not in the way. We're glad you're here." Val carries the pot to the waiting hot pad on the kitchen table. "I made grits and eggs and a sausage veggie hash."

"That sounds great. Thank you."

Val's husband, Micah, walks into the kitchen carrying his favorite mug, a large blue Yellowstone National Park mug, no doubt filled with black coffee. No one could accuse Micah of having a sweet tooth. He's a lawyer and he's handling the insurance and some other little details to do with the fire. Could I do it myself? Absolutely. But I'd thrown my arms around my brother-in-law when he'd offered. If there's anyone I can trust, it's Micah.

He and his relationship with Val make me feel ... jealous isn't the word. It's more like a feeling of missing out. They're an amazing team and I want that. Someone to love and trust. Someone who will have my back, like I'd have his. I think a new goal for the time the restaurant is closed is to find a kind, local man to love. Both those qualifiers are a must. He needs to be kind, and he needs to live here. Or maybe one town over would be okay.

Also, dark hair wouldn't hurt.

"Mornin' Ivy. Good to see you up and around." Micah smiles as he takes his seat at the table.

"Alright. It's not that crazy that I'm up."

Val and Micah give me nearly identical looks of dissent.

"It's not." I make myself a water and turn to find Juniper and her younger brother, Peter, sitting at the table.

"I almost forgot you lived here," Peter says, eyeing Ivy over his orange juice. Juniper snickers.

Oh, good grief. "I ate dinner with you guys *last night*."

"Yeah, but you did that sometimes before. Breakfast is for people who live here," Juniper says with a smirk.

"I'll try to make it down for breakfast from now on so nobody forgets about me."

"Go, Pete! Go!"

Peter is a fast swimmer for a seven-year-old. He's in lane four and is only inches behind the winner as they approach the wall.

"You know he can't hear you, right?" Juniper asks from her spot on my right.

"You're being awfully sassy to me today. Everyone here is yelling." I watch as Peter narrowly misses out on the win, then jump down from my place on the bleachers to go congratulate him.

"Parents need to wait at the bleachers." A middle-aged man holds up his hand toward me.

"Good thing I'm not his parent. Spinster aunt here." I attempt to win him over with humor, then try to walk around him. I have nothing to lose.

"Spinster aunts need to wait too. It's for the safety of our swimmers. We've had too many people by the pool before, resulting in people being pushed in."

"Fine." I'm not unreasonable. I turn back to find my family laughing at me. Gee thanks, guys. I didn't know the rules.

"Anizey! Did you see how fast I was going? I almost won!" Peter's a bundle of energy as he runs up to me. I lean down to hug him, immediately regretting it as water soaks through my white shirt. Perfect.

"I sure did, Buddy! You were amazing. I bet you'll go even faster next race." I put my arm around his shoulders as we walk to the bleachers. What's a little more water?

"I know, but I won't be here for the next race," Peter pouts.

"Yes, but we will be in England! Maybe while we're there, we can watch some videos of Michael Phelps in the London Olympics. That would be cool, huh?"

Peter looks at me, confused. "Who's Michael Phelps?"

3

Alexander

"I don't have time to go to England," I say, knowing full well that I do have time. I finished the publicity circuit for *The Mark of Everlore*, it premiered, and now I'm taking a break. I don't necessarily feel like I need a break, but they say it's healthy to take them. I plan to visit my Napa vacation house and lounge around, not go home to England to deal with my aunt's solicitor, Mr. Crawley.

"Her will is very clear. If you want your grandfather's box, you have to come and follow the stipulations she set forth in her letter to you."

"What's in this box?" I sit in my usual chair facing my large living room windows.

"She doesn't specify, only says it's filled with treasures you will want." Mr. Crawley sounds like he regrets having to do this to me.

I sigh. "And you can't read me the letter with the stipulations? I have to come get it?"

"I'm afraid so."

I sigh. "Alright. I'll think about it. If I decide to come, I'll have my assistant get in touch with your office." I end the call and set my phone down, looking out the window at the ocean, the Malibu sand down below. What kind of rubbish is this? I'd say I'm surprised, but I'm not. My aunt was always seventy percent eccentric, thirty percent insane. She tried to physically attack me once. While she gave a valiant effort, I'm six foot two and had been training for a role where I played a boxer at the time. Still, I learned not to offer any differing opinions of the monarchy in her presence.

I'm the only one left in my family now; Aunt Agnes never had any children. My parents are gone and I don't have siblings. It makes sense that if she had anything to leave behind, she would leave it to me, but this? It would be just like her to leave me a box of wadded-up sandwich wrappers and lead me on a wild goose chase to get it.

I decide against going, instead choosing to make this lunacy wait until I'm next in England. Or more likely, I won't deal with it at all. I push it from my mind and hop into my Bentley Bentayga.

I drive half an hour to Thousand Oaks to eat at my favorite restaurant—a little diner that serves breakfast all day—before their dinner rush. I love going there. It's owned by Mr. and Mrs. Parker, a lovely couple in their mid-fifties. I've known them for almost five years now, and they've become special to me. I didn't realize what I was missing in Hollywood until I got to know them. At first, I liked that they didn't watch TV or movies, so they didn't recognize me. I still love that, but it's become more.

It's not that I mind being famous. I don't necessarily like it, but I know it comes with the territory, so I deal with it. I enjoy acting. And I love being a part of such a huge creation. Ultimately, I'd like to be a screenwriter.

But it's nice to be somewhere and just be me. To avoid people fawning over me, asking me for autographs and photos. I generally oblige the fans because I understand the urge, but it's so nice simply to be Alexander.

"Alexander! It's been too long. I almost texted." Mrs. Parker greets me at the register.

"I'm sorry. I've been working a lot. It really has been too long." I smile, filled with fondness for this kind woman, along with her husband. "I'm glad to be back."

She reaches up and pats me on the cheek. "I'm glad you're back too, sweet boy. Now, tell me how you want to fill your belly today."

I can still feel the warmth of her hand on my cheek, like she infuses her touch with love and leaves her mark everywhere she means to. I still remember being shocked the first time she did it to me. It's like a hug she can give while staying behind the counter.

"You know what? Surprise me."

Mrs. Parker grins. "I know just the thing." She rings up my order. "It's on the house."

"No. No. That's very kind, but—"

"Ah, ah. No arguing. I will spoil you if I want to."

I've learned it's fruitless to argue with Mrs. Parker, so I do as I always do and slip a fifty into the tip jar as soon as she turns her back. I always end up spending more when she gives it to me on the house, and I'm always glad.

I slide onto the worn black vinyl of my usual booth in the corner, and she meets me there with a cup of hot tea and water. She knows I always end up asking for water too. They had begun stocking English breakfast tea, since my second visit, when I told her I fancied a cup of tea. I hadn't the heart to tell them the tea they had chosen was dreadful. I simply add plenty of cream and sugar, and smile. Then refuse refills.

"Thank you."

"Of course, sweetheart. I'll be back soon with your food. And you let me know if you need more tea."

"I will. Thank you."

I will not.

I pull out my phone as I wait, hoping to see reviews of *The Mark of Everlore*, but instead the headlines are about me and Crescent—our chemistry, and how Grey Blankenship might feel about it. It takes a surprising amount of scrolling before I find what I'm looking for.

"Here you go!" Mrs. Parker says, startling me and causing me to hide my phone like I'd been up to something. She laughs at me fondly. "Okay. I brought you two eggs—over easy—my homemade sausage, I know you like that. And strawberry French toast with extra whipped cream."

"It looks amazing. I couldn't have ordered better myself." It truly does look delicious, but I'm suddenly struck with a thought that leaves me with an odd sadness, and it can only be because I've been asked to go back home.

I can't remember the last time I had baked beans for breakfast.

I'm lost in my thoughts as I robotically make my way inside my house. Why was that solicitor just now calling me? Aunt Agnes died months ago. I'd gone home for her funeral, but it was during filming. I stepped off the plane, attended the funeral, and stepped back on. Otherwise, I hadn't been home in probably two years.

I grew up in England, splitting time between our countryside estate, which I sold after my parents' fatal collision, and the home in the Knightsbridge neighborhood of London. My aunt was angry with me when I sold the country estate. She said I was forgetting about England and the things that are truly important. I maintain that this is not accurate, but I regret selling the estate. It seemed like a waste for it to sit there, and at the time it served as a reminder of my father's disappointment. Instead of stepping into the life he planned for me, I moved and became an actor. Now that more time has passed, I feel nostalgic for the time spent there in my youth. I can't dwell on that; there's no getting it back now.

The home in Knightsbridge is currently occupied by the staff. I told them I trust them and as long as the house stays in great condition, I don't care what they do. They have it ready for me anytime I let them know I'm coming, welcoming me like a long-lost son.

I let out a sigh as I sit on my navy leather sofa and pull out my phone to ask my assistant, Mark, to make the plans.

4

IVY

IF I GO THE most direct route, and I usually do, driving to the restaurant from my sister's house takes me past our childhood home. I'm practical and usually do what is most efficient, but today I'm driving the long way. I'm not in the mood for a walk down memory lane.

I'm hit with memories anyway, as I drive by our middle school. I see Val. Her dead eyes and defeated posture as she dragged her backpack to my twenty-year-old Buick. I'd picked her up an hour after she was supposed to be picked up. She had a club meeting after school, and mom assured us she would pick her up. I don't know why either of us believed her. She'd given us no reason to; she was as unreliable as she was uncaring. All her care and attention went outside our family. I played basketball all throughout high school. She made it to one game. One. The boosters were fundraising, so the important school people were there. She needed to make an appearance.

We'd never known our father, but I always believed living with him would be better than raising Val on my own. I was never able to figure out who he was.

I pull up to the back of the restaurant, and a tear escapes as I look up at the window of my apartment where my dainty white curtain used to hang. I glance at the notebook in the passenger seat. My plan had been to look around now that the space had been totally cleaned out. I'd thought I would finalize my notes and plans and get everything to my contractor. But I don't think I can go in. The thought of seeing it sitting there empty is too much. I'm still not over seeing it just after the fire.

Still, I'm overwhelmed. There's so much to do. I need to get the ball rolling. Not only am I missing out on a paycheck while it's closed, but many of my employees are taking time off until I reopen, finding work here and there when they can, for a little cash. I'm suddenly overwhelmed by the responsibility of it.

And I'm struck again with the need for a partner. Even if he isn't involved in the restaurant at all, just to have him in my corner. And hugs. I love hugs. I always thought I would be fine on my own, but it's hard to hug yourself.

My practical side decides to fight for dominance. I'm about to be gone for two weeks. I need to get things going so work can happen while I'm gone. I glance at the apartment window and decide to see this as the opportunity it is. I can take this blank slate and make it into something even better than it was. Maybe I would like to have a partner in this, but I don't necessarily need one. It's gonna be great.

—ele—

"Anizey! Do you have Scuffy?" Juniper calls from her room down the hall.

"Why would I have your bear?" I call back, adding a pair of shorts to my suitcase and checking off my list.

Juniper doesn't answer. The house is in the typical pre-vacation chaos. Mom may not have taken care of us, but she did take us on vacations—an impressive person needs impressive family photos—so the pre-vacation chaos is a familiar feeling.

I create a new list of items to get in the morning. Charger. Toothbrush. Hairbrush. Book. That's it. It's a short list, but I feel better having it.

"Can you help Peter pare down the plane entertainment he's taking?" Val asks, sticking her head in my room. "I'm sure you're basically packed, and I am not at all ready."

She's not wrong. Sometimes I think I spoiled my sister a bit by doing so much for her for too long. And being the person who kept her on track for whatever she needed to be doing.

"Sure thing. Is he packed otherwise?"

"Yeah. I packed him yesterday. Stop looking at me like you're proud. I'm a fully functioning adult who has kept two children alive, well, and happy for over nine years now."

I laugh, not having realized I'd made any sort of face. "I know you have and you're great at it."

"Thank you, and thanks for helping. He stopped listening to me and I couldn't give any more time explaining why we can't take twenty picture books or slime on an airplane."

"I'll do my best," I say with a flourish as I zip my suitcase.

"Have either of you seen my toothbrush?" asks Juniper.

"Shouldn't it be where you left it after brushing your teeth this morning?" her mother asks.

"You would think," Juniper says, looking unsure.

"Go look again, honey."

Val is letting Juniper pack her own bag for the first time. She's thrilled, but I plan to take a look in the bag after she goes to bed.

I can't help it.

When the kids are packed and in their pajamas, they ask me to read their bedtime story. When they fight over whose turn it is to choose the book, I tell them that it's my turn. I pull *Peter Pan* from the shelf and read to them about three children who live in London, and caution them against sleeping with the window open while we're there.

5

ALEXANDER

"WHAT DO YOU MEAN there will be hints and riddles?" I'm generally up for things, and if it were anyone else who had set up this … game? I don't even know what to call it … I would gladly go along and have a great time. But this is Aunt Agnes. I simply cannot fathom the insanity I am about to step into.

"Once you solve a riddle or figure out a hint, you will take a photo of yourself at the location she has sent you to. Send the photo to me and you will receive the next clue after a prescribed amount of time," Mr. Crawley says as he leans back in his high-backed leather chair.

I blow out a breath, hoping it doesn't reach him across his wide mahogany desk. "So, she's stretching this out? I can't just knock it out and be on my way with my grandfather's box?"

"I'm afraid that's correct. The good news is, I can give you the first clue today and you can get started."

I stare at him, wondering how any of this is good news. "How big is this box?"

"Bigger than a shoebox, smaller than a fridge." He gives the smallest smile before schooling his features. There's a bit of him that is enjoying this. He's smart not having the box sitting out. I'd be tempted to nick it and run.

"Might I ask, why are you just now getting around t—. Never mind, I know why. Aunt Agnes said to wait a certain amount of time after her funeral, didn't she?"

"She did indeed, sir."

I've got to get out of this office; it smells like dust and hundreds of years' worth of pipe tobacco. "Alright. Give me the first riddle, I suppose."

He slides a piece of paper across his desk like we are in the middle of some sort of negotiation. "My mobile is on there. Best of luck."

I look down at the paper where my first riddle awaits.

> You wore a special hat
> On your mother's lap, you sat
> A milestone, but not for you
> Out of frame, but I'm there too

The riddle and the long day of travel combine, making me close my eyes. "I'm too knackered for this."

I step into the foyer of my London home and, as if she were staring out the window waiting, I'm met almost immediately by the housekeeper, Mrs. Brown. Before making the transition to housekeeper, she had been my nanny, and she has a hard time remembering I am no longer the child who would sneak sticky buns and leave evidence of my crime all over the house.

"Master Alexander! How good it is to see you. Welcome home." Mrs. Brown moves in to hug me but stops. "I apologize, Mr. Henry. I got carried away."

"You don't need to apologize to me. Especially not for a hug. I almost always fancy a nice hug." I set down my suitcase and Mr. Brown—Mrs. Brown's husband and the butler—who I had not heard approach, takes it and heads for the stairs with a muttered "Sir." A man of few words. I wrap my arms around Mrs. Brown and squeeze just like I used to.

She smiles as I release her, patting my arm like I imagine a grandmother would.

"And please just call me Alexander. When you call me Mr. Henry, I think you're talking to my father."

"Alright, alright, but you know Mrs. Henry wouldn't be

pleased."

"Ah, let's give mum the benefit of the doubt. I like to think she would have softened as she aged. Yeah?"

"Perhaps you're right ... Alexander."

I grin at my old friend, and despite my fatigue and deep desire for my bed, I put my arm around her shoulders and lead her toward the kitchen. "Now, tell me. What's been going on with you?"

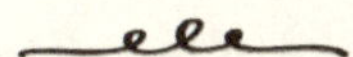

I wake the next morning, only to find it's actually afternoon. Five a.m. in LA. Still, I'm rested and ready to get on with my first riddle. Mrs. Brown is nowhere to be seen, but she left me a tray of pastries, a tea service—its kettle now cold—and a note asking me to let her know when I'm up and she can cook a warm breakfast.

I let her keep doing whatever is currently occupying her; I'm sure I can find something in the fridge.

Warm tea, soft-boiled eggs, and two Danish pastries in hand, I sit at the small table where my mum always enjoyed her morning tea. It's by a window and overlooks the small garden behind the house. I pull out the riddle and, for the first time, truly ponder it.

I wore a special hat? I can't remember wearing a special hat.

I wear hats now when I'm trying to conceal my identity. But ... I was in my mother's lap, so I would have had to have been small. Is she trying to send me somewhere I went when I was small for a special occasion? She thought I would remember that?

My gaze is drawn to my mother's row of hydrangea bushes; their beautiful white blossoms would have made Mum happy. They make me smile. And I realize this is the first time I've been here since their death that the memory of her, of them, has brought happiness instead of mourning. They may have been strict, and often demanding, but there was always the strong undercurrent of their love threaded throughout it all.

6

IVY

WE ARRIVED IN LONDON yesterday, and despite our efforts to avoid jet lag, not a soul in our hotel suite was awake until after lunchtime. Deciding we needed to get up and move, I woke them. I was met by a range of reactions, from Peter's excitement to Val's pillow being launched at my face.

Still, I was successful. We're out. All of us enjoying the sunshine in Wandsworth Park. I think it was a good move. The warm breeze on my skin makes me smile as I watch the kids on the swings from where Val and I sit on a bench.

"This was a good idea," Val says, her eyes on her husband as he plays like he is going to steal Peter's shoes when he swings forward.

"I know."

"Don't get cocky, you weren't the only one with this good idea."

In the ten minutes since our arrival, it seems everyone within a five-mile radius has decided to visit Wandsworth Park on this beautiful day. "Let's give the kids a few more minutes, then go for a walk," I suggest.

"Sounds good."

Micah and the kids play for five more minutes, until Juniper declares, "We should go for a walk."

"That was easy," Val says to me as we get up from the bench.

The park is beautiful. It runs along the River Thames, and we pause briefly at the railing to watch the river pass by. The walkway is lined by huge, beautiful trees. They remind me of a tree in Val and Micah's yard. It's some kind of sycamore, maybe these are too. Whatever they are, they make for a stunning walk.

We've been walking a while when I turn to say something to Peter and don't see him behind me.

"Where's Peter?"

My sister looks frantically around. "I thought he was walking behind us with Micah." She turns to where her husband and Juniper walk behind her. They are both oblivious, talking to each other. "Where's Peter?"

"I thought ..." Micah looks at each of them and the surrounding area. "I don't see him."

"Oh my gosh, he's been snatched!" Panic swells in Val's eyes.

"He has not been snatched. We'll find him. He can't be far," I assure her, despite feeling similarly. I rub my hands up and down her upper arms.

"We have our phones," Micah says. "I'll take Juniper and we'll walk back toward the park. Honey, you keep walking ahead, and, Ivy, why don't you walk inward through the trees?" He walks to Val and hugs her tightly, but briefly. "We'll find him."

I watch as Micah turns to the river, shuddering to think what could be if that were the direction Peter had gone.

Trying not to pick up any more of my sister's panic, I pass under the trees and see some kids playing soccer ... excuse me, football. A couple of minutes later, I'm almost hit in the head with a frisbee. My search leads me around way too many picnickers. As my panic builds, my eyes are darting all over the place when I round a tree and crash right into someone. I know at this point I surely look deeply worried, maybe even crazed. I thought for sure I would have found him by now or would have received a call that one of them had.

The stranger reaches out for my shoulders, keeping me from flying onto the grass.

"Miss, are you alright?"

The electricity of his touch hits me before I look up. When I do, I'm met with gorgeous slate-blue eyes. It takes a moment, but eventually I realize the stunning man with his hands on my shoulders is Alexander Henry. The movie star. He's wearing a hat and eyeglasses as if to disguise himself, but it's not terribly effective.

"I'm fine. I'm so sorry." It's shockingly hard to do so, but I turn to continue with my frantic searching, and hear his footsteps jogging up behind me.

"I apologize, but you don't seem fine."

I stop and look up at him once again. I'm not one to be impressed with him being an actor, but even in my slightly crazed state, I can admit he is even more handsome in person.

"I'm ..." I breathe deeply, trying to calm myself, and find comfort in the eyes of the man standing across from me. "I'm looking for my nephew. He's seven and he went missing about ten minutes ago. I've got to keep looking."

I step away, but he stops me with a gentle hand on my arm. "What does he look like? What's he wearing? I'll help."

My first instinct was to say no and walk away, but what would it hurt for him to help? I pull out my phone and show him the photo I took of the kids on the playground.

"It's hard to tell in the photo, but that's a dinosaur on his shirt. His name is Peter."

"Got it. Do you think he went back to the playground?"

"Maybe, but my brother-in-law went that way. I was given this middle area to search." I start walking, and he steps in beside me. It feels good to have his eyes on the task too.

We've been searching for five minutes or so, but it feels like so much longer. Alexander Henry touching my back or shoulder every once in a while, as if to say, "I'm here, we'll find him." It helps keep me calm until I let my thoughts run wild with the passage of so much time. I stop walking and check my phone for a missed call. Nothing. My breathing becomes rapid, and a tear escapes my eye. I see Alexander Henry reach, as if he were going to wipe the tear from my cheek, but he stops himself.

"Oh no. None of this. We'll find him, or his parents will. Kidnappings are rare."

"But they happen." My bottom lip trembles, briefly drawing his attention.

"Come here." He opens his arms, and despite him being a stranger, I step into them, needing a few seconds of calm.

He soothes me with his hands against my upper back, the pressure of his arms around me, and the cadence of his words as he reassures me. I take a deep breath as I step back from this surprising man.

"Thank you."

He nods. "Ready to resume looking?"

"Yes."

We've been back looking and calling for Peter for less than a minute when Alexander nudges my arm and points toward the group of boys playing soccer. "Is that him?"

Relief like I've never felt washes over me. I had missed him when I had looked before. "Yes," I say as I turn, resting my forehead on Alexander Henry's shoulder while I take a deep breath to collect myself. I don't want to go over there and lash out at my nephew. I'm sure he didn't mean to cause the worry that he did. He saw a soccer ball and had to make friends with the kids playing with it. He needs to understand the problem with what happened, but I'll leave that to his parents.

I lift my head from Alexander Henry's shoulder, deciding to call Val before going to collect Peter. The movie star is giving me a bit of a funny, yet still friendly, look. I suppose it is really weird that I had my head on him. Of course, he did hug me earlier. It can't be that weird.

"I found him. Come to the grass area." I end the call on Val's relieved sob and turn to Peter's true finder. I stare up at him for a moment. "Thank you for helping me."

"I was glad to." He looks at me like I'm a puzzle, pausing to look at my hair. I'm sure my wild curls have done nothing to help my crazy-lady appearance.

"I promise I haven't just escaped from an insane asylum."

"I wasn't thinking that, but now that you've mentioned it, I'm sure that's exactly what you've done." He looks entirely serious. Those acting skills are coming in handy.

I grin up at him, and I swear his pupils dilate. "I bet you

regret going for a walk today now that you know the truth."

"Oh yes. I'll be riddled with regret for years to come."

"Good. I like to make a lasting impression." I glance over to make sure Peter is still playing soccer. Football.

His fingertips touch my jaw, gently urging my gaze back toward his. His voice is low when he speaks. "You've definitely made a lasting impression on me."

I swallow and stare up at Alexander Henry for a moment. "I ... umm ... thank you. I'm going to go get Peter."

"Okay."

I smile like this was it—all that was to be for Alexander Henry and me—and walk toward my nephew. Only, it isn't long before I hear footsteps jogging behind me once again.

7

ALexander

I HANG BACK WATCHING the reunion of Peter and his parents. I could have left. Maybe I should have, but there is just something intriguing about this woman whose name I haven't even gotten. Her hair is a dozen different colors, ranging from rich brown to gold, with her wild curls really showing off in the sunshine. Then there were her pale green eyes when she first really looked at me. They were captivating and best of all, they didn't show a hint of recognition. To be fair, she was in the middle of something pretty important, but still.

She looks over her shoulder and finds me watching. I smile because I have no shame. She walks over to me, and I take the opportunity to check her out, starting with her white sneakers, moving up over her sage green sundress, finally landing on her beautiful face. She's giving me a crooked smile and shaking her head.

"I saw that," she says as she reaches my side.

"I wanted you to."

She shakes her head and smiles again, looking back toward her family. "Thanks again. I had seen those boys playing soccer—"

"Football."

"Yes, I know." She rolls her eyes at me, and I love it. "Anyway, I had seen them, but had somehow missed that he was with them. So I'm glad I ran into you. Literally."

"Me too." So glad. "And I'm glad I was able to help. I don't have any little ones in my life, but I know that must have been incredibly scary."

"Yeah, it's not something I'm aching to relive."

We stand in silence for a moment, her eyes back on her family. "Might I ask your name?"

She looks back up at me and the way the sun hits her face would make a Hollywood light designer faint at the beauty. "I'm Ivy." She extends her hand to shake, and I shock myself by bringing it to my lips and kissing it gently. Maybe I've lived in the U.S. for too long.

"A pleasure to meet you, beautiful Ivy."

She holds back a smile, and I can tell she is doing her best not to be charmed. "Is this an English thing, or is this just who you are?" Definitely not an English thing.

I shrug. "Aren't you going to ask for my name?"

"Will you expect me to kiss your hand if I do?"

This draws out a surprised laugh from me. "It's a requirement here in England. When you meet someone, but only learn their name later, you must kiss their hand upon introduction."

"That is an interesting custom. Clearly, I have a lot to learn."

"Clearly you do."

"One thing I don't need to learn is your name."

I place my hand over my heart. "That hurts. Not to mention that you won't know how to label the contact when you put my number in your phone."

"You're awfully presumptuous, Alexander Henry."

I squint at her accusingly. "So you know who I am."

"I do live on Earth."

She's funny. "It's just not impressive to you that I'm a famous actor?"

"I'm not saying you aren't great at what you do. I've just never been one to think celebrities are any more important than anyone else. I mean, my brother-in-law is great at his job, but does anyone know who he is? Or care? No."

Ah, okay, this I can work with. This I kind of like. I'm about to respond when the girl, Peter's sister, I assume, walks over.

"Hey, mister. I'm Juniper."

"Hello, Juniper. Lovely to meet you. I'm Alexander."

"Ohh! A real English person! The only one we've met so far was at the hotel and he was cranky. And didn't really talk to us."

"Alexander is the one who found Peter," Ivy says as her sister and brother-in-law walk up with Peter.

Peter looks thoroughly chastised and doesn't look in my direction, but both his parents do a double take. I laugh, then elbow Ivy lightly in the ribs. "Some people are impressed," I whisper toward her. "I take it my disguise isn't working," I say to the group.

"You should grow a handlebar mustache," Ivy suggests, the glint in her eye making my smile grow.

I extend my hand to the sister. "Hello, I'm Alexander." Then to her husband—we shake, and then he introduces himself and his wife, who is openly staring, her gaze bouncing around between me and her sister.

"A pleasure meeting you both. I was wondering, could I borrow Ivy for a bit?"

Her gaze, which had previously been on the children, swings up to me. "What?" she asks, eyes wide.

"Of course you can," her sister, Val, answers.

Ivy turns on her sister. "Excuse me? You'd send me off with a stranger?"

"You'll be fine." She shrugs and grins, then turns to me. "We have dinner reservations at six; maybe have her back to the hotel by five?"

"Y'all stop talking about me like I'm not here."

"Would you like to take a walk with me, Ivy?" I ask.

She shakes her head and smiles at me, because apparently that's the only reaction I can elicit from her. I make it my goal to get at least one smile *without* a shaking head.

"Sure. Let's walk."

"I'll buy my own ice cream," Ivy insists as we stand in line inside an old-fashioned ice cream parlor. We'd walked to the far side of the park and continued onward into the streets where we found this place. I learned that she's from the foothills of North Carolina. She owns a restaurant that recently burnt down, and she hates cockroaches. I still don't understand how *that* fact even came up.

"I insist. You owe me this honor," I begin, and she raises her eyebrows. "Because I found Peter."

She laughs and shakes her head. "Are you sure? Because I plan on getting a waffle cone. That's extra."

"I think I can swing that. You could even get a second scoop."

"Wow. Maybe you *are* impressive." She pats my shoulder

and steps to the counter.

She orders her raspberry vanilla waffle cone and I order my pistachio in a cup and we go sit at an outdoor table.

Her hair calls to me, and I reach up to twirl a curl on my finger, but she bats me away.

"What are you doing?"

"Remember, I found Peter."

"You already said that once and I'm afraid that's all you get." She shrugs. "You should have used it more wisely."

She is so cute. I want to count her freckles. "Okay. But just so you know, you can touch my hair anytime."

"Thank you for that kind offer. Your hat is blocking the way though, and if you took it off, you'd have hat hair, and I'm not going to touch hat hair. So I guess not."

"What I'm hearing you say is I shouldn't wear a hat next time I see you." In my periphery, I see a group of women staring. I angle said hat down, although I'm not sure it helps. We were stopped three times in the park, and the teenage boy who made our ice cream stuttered and shook. Maybe it wasn't in response to me, but for his sake, I hope it was.

"You think there should be a next time? I'm not sure how your girlfriend would feel about that." She licks her cone and I have to avert my eyes.

"Ah. Well, you see ... this can't go any further than this table, but our relationship isn't real. Our agents set it up. I like her very much; she's become a close friend, but that's it. She's actually seeing someone she went to high school with. And she isn't really my type."

Ivy squints her eyes at me as if she were trying to use x-ray vision to see the truth. "I thought Grey Blankenship was everyone's type."

"I'm more interested in women who are not easily impressed. With wild curls and bright emerald eyes." I take a bite of my ice cream.

She nods. "That's oddly specific. Good luck with that search."

"I have a good feeling about it." I do. But I can't help but think about our geographical differences. Since moving to Hollywood, I always assumed I would end up with someone who lived out that way. That would be simple, and if Ivy wasn't so intriguing, I might simply tell her it was nice meeting her and go about my business. But there is something about her that tells me she might be worth whatever compromise or concession I'd have to make in order to keep her in my life. Or try to.

We finish our ice cream and continue walking and talking, ending up at her hotel. I don't want to let her go, but it's the end of the road for me for now.

"It's been an absolute pleasure," I say, hoping she sees how much I mean it. "Could I have your number?"

"What for?" She smiles. She is giving me a hard time.

"So perhaps I'll have the chance to look into those beautiful green eyes again."

I am sitting in what had been our family's favorite room in our house. It was where we watched movies and hung out together. It was also where mum had an entire wall covered in family photos. The rest of the house was dedicated to art and cultivated design, but the living room was ours.

I stand to look through the pictures, assuming the pain of their loss will come, but like this morning, I found happiness upon seeing them.

A photo in a simple gold frame catches my eye and I do a double take. I'm maybe two years old, wearing a party hat. I'm sitting in Mum's lap, and she looks so carefree and beautiful. If I was two, this must have been her thirtieth birthday. This is the answer to the first riddle. It's a restaurant nearby that we went to frequently growing up and would go to almost every time I came home to visit.

I snap a photo and send it to Mr. Crawley. He informs me that I actually have to go to the places when I solve the riddles. After dinner, I do so, but I'm not immediately given the next one. He'd said it may not be right away, so while I'm not surprised, I *am* disappointed. Instead of having a new riddle to ponder, I'm left with only thoughts of the mesmerizing Ivy to keep me company. I needed the riddle to keep me from getting in touch with her too soon.

8

IVY

WE'RE EATING DINNER IN a dimly lit pub close to our hotel. Earlier, when I'd arrived back at the hotel, I'd avoided talking about the afternoon, ducking into the bathroom to get ready. I wasn't ready to talk. I needed to sort through my feelings. Still do, but as I lower my menu, having taken as long as a person possibly can to look at a two-page, well-spaced list of food, I meet my sister's hazel eyes.

"Alright. You cannot keep us in suspense any longer. Tell us all about it. Was he as nice as they make him seem? What did he say? Tell us everything."

I sigh. And before I can speak, Juniper jumps in. "Is he strong like that superhero he played in that movie?"

"You haven't even seen *that movie*." I laugh. "I have no

evidence to say he is strong like a superhero." At Juniper's disappointment, I add. "I also have no evidence that he isn't."

"I bet he is. Did you see how big he is? And he's taller than Dad. And Dad is tall!"

"I did notice." It was hard not to. And how he thinks wearing a hat and glasses will disguise him in the least is beyond me. But I guess you have to try. "He was extremely nice and seemed genuine. He was a good listener and asked good questions, like he actually cared about what I had to say. Honestly, that was the most surprising thing. I assumed someone like him would be a bit self-important."

"Why did he want to go on a walk with you?" Val asks, then we all pause as our server sets our drinks on the table. "Thank you."

"The better question is, why *wouldn't* he want to go on a walk with me?" I joke.

"Because you're a girl and he doesn't know you at all," Peter supplies, helpfully.

His parents laugh, but I look at him seriously. "That's a good point."

"This is crazy. You'll never forget the day you met Alexander Henry," Val says, shaking her head.

"It may not just be a day. He asked for my number."

"What?" My sister exclaims at the same time Micah says, "Are you serious?"

I nodded. "Who knows, he might get in touch. He might not." I shrug like it doesn't matter, and really I know it doesn't. There is nowhere we could go beyond London acquaintances. But I enjoyed spending time with him, and I'm not gonna lie, it felt good to have such a handsome man show interest in me.

Of course, I didn't give him a lot of reason to contact me. I did my typical. Gave him attitude in an effort to protect myself. I've spent my adult life thinking I'd be better on my own. I couldn't imagine putting my trust in someone, until recently, that is. Still, I'm not certain it's the right move for me. And if it is, I know it isn't with someone who lives across the Atlantic.

"Are you gonna call him?" Val asks.

"He didn't give me his number." Probably because I didn't ask.

—ele—

"Let's walk to see Big Ben," I suggest. "It's always pretty at night in the movies."

We're standing outside the pub, each of us knowing we are far from sleep. The five-hour time difference will probably get us until we leave. Even the kids are bouncing up and down. Eight p.m. at home and they are both dragging. Eight p.m. here and they're ready to run a 5k.

So am I. Part of it is the time change, and part is nervous

energy, wondering if Alexander will get in touch.

Everyone agrees to the walk, and we set off. I marvel at the architecture. The mix of extremely old and ultra-modern. And some buildings that were likely ultra-modern fifty years ago. Something about the combination is so visually stimulating and exciting to me. Maybe it's the novelty.

We pass by a classic red phone booth, and I wonder how often it's actually used for phone calls these days. Currently, there's a group of college-age kids taking photos in it.

I'm taken by surprise as we come to Westminster Abbey. I hadn't seen it on the map. I want to come back and see it during the day. A quick search tells me it opened in 1269 and I cannot believe they were able to build something so incredibly impressive back then. I once had a professor say that as humans we are getting dumber. That as our technology increases, our intelligence decreases. I'm not sure if he meant that as correlation or causation, or if he was correct, but it's interesting to think about.

"There's Big Benny!" Peter calls out as we come around a curve and Big Ben comes into view. He clearly thought it would be hilarious to rename the famous clock tower after his stuffed dinosaur named Benny.

We cross the street into a grassy area to look up at the giant clock. It is really cool to see in person. The lights on the building and the illuminated clock faces take me back to *Peter*

Pan and it makes me so very thankful our Peter didn't go off to Neverland today.

The kids are quickly bored, so after taking a few photos, we decide to take one of those classic double-decker buses back to the hotel. We got seats up top, and you would have thought the kids were riding on Santa's sleigh, for all the excitement that brought.

It's hours later and I can't sleep. Midnight is only seven at home. I've been tossing in this bed for an hour. I should probably just get up for a bit. Instead, I lie there and pick up my phone.

9

ALEXANDER

IT'S MIDNIGHT AND, OF course, I'm wide awake. I normally wouldn't go to bed for another seven hours or so. It gets harder to adjust every time I come home. So instead of being in bed, I'm sitting in the living room, staring at the new riddle on my phone.

> A connection, it does make
> But not over a lake
> Confusion with a song
> But you might have it wrong

"Oh! I'm an idiot," I yell.

Mr. Brown rushes into the room, apparently having been

nearby. "Sir? Are you alright?"

"Yes, I'm sorry. I was just calling myself an idiot."

"Carry on, then." I didn't miss his tiny, cheeky smile as he turned from the room. He acts like he doesn't care, but I know he does. Wonder why he's up at this hour.

I head to bed, where instead of tossing and turning, I pick up my phone again. I'll leave Ivy a message for her to see when she wakes up.

ALEXANDER

Good morning, beautiful Ivy.

ALEXANDER

It's Alexander. I've been thinking about you and would love to see you tomorrow (or today, if you're reading this when I assume you will.)

Three dots start dancing above the keyboard. She's up!

BEAUTIFUL IVY

Can't sleep either?

ALEXANDER

Nope. Haven't got on London time just yet.

ALEXANDER

So… tomorrow?

BEAUTIFUL IVY

I came on this vacation with my family. I can't just abandon them. But maybe you could join us for some sightseeing tomorrow afternoon? I know it might be boring to a local, but plan to go to the London Eye and London Bridge. I mean, who knows what we'll get up to, but that's the plan.

Perfect. I need to go to Tower Bridge. I wonder if she knows she's going to Tower Bridge. I'm sure she doesn't actually mean London Bridge.

ALEXANDER

It's a date.

BEAUTIFUL IVY

Is it, though?

ALEXANDER

It is in my mind.

ALEXANDER

Do you think you'll be falling asleep soon?

BEAUTIFUL IVY

No. I'm not tired enough, and you're making my mind spin.

I'm making her mind spin. I love it.

ALEXANDER

Am I? *Grinning emoji*

ALEXANDER

Can I give you a ring?

BEAUTIFUL IVY

I assume you're not meaning a physical ring… so sure.

I shift to sit against my headboard, then hit call. She takes her time answering, and it makes me wonder what she's doing.

"Hello." There's a grittiness to her voice that wasn't there this afternoon. I want to hear her every time she sounds like this. What is it about this woman? I've never felt this kind of unexplainable need to be near someone. And for this to happen with someone who doesn't make sense? Someone I basically know nothing about, who lives across the country from me. If I stepped outside of myself and looked at the situation, I'd think I was crackers.

"Hello. Did you all have a nice dinner?" I ask, trying to collect my thoughts. What am I doing? What's the purpose of this call? To me pursuing her at all?

"We did. I had authentic fish and chips for the first time, and let me tell you, it's a good thing I don't live here. That's the only thing I would ever want to eat."

"Even for breakfast?"

"Sure. I'd turn it into small fish bites with hash browns. But it would basically be the same."

"I guess it's good for your health that you aren't here indefinitely. How long *will* you be here?"

"Nine more days."

"What will you do when you get home? What is your typical day?"

"Well, when I get home, I'll be dealing with renovations from the fire. So not really what I do on a typical day."

"I'm sure that's difficult and frustrating, but maybe it's a chance to start again and fix things that you didn't love before? I don't know. Just trying to find something positive about it. Which is easy for me to say." What am I doing? Stop babbling.

"I still wish it hadn't happened, but I'm glad I can make some improvements. I thought ... I might as well."

"Definitely. So once it's up and running again, will you be there most days? Are you the owner *and* manager? Or do you manage from afar? I'm friends with a couple who own a restaurant, and there is always one of them there. It seems like a lot of work."

"It definitely is. Ultimately, I'd love to have managers I trust to take over a lot of the time, but I have a little trouble with that. With turning over something so important to me. It's a lot for me."

"You have trouble trusting people?"

"Yeah. I have trouble feeling like I can count on people. It was probably five years before I felt like I could really trust Micah."

"For what it's worth, I've always been very dependable."

Ivy laughs. "That's good to know. Maybe in five years, I'll agree."

"I hope it doesn't take quite that long." I smile as I hear her moving around on her bed. At least that's what I assume is happening. "I love your accent."

"You know, I was fixin' to say the same thing to you. And just your voice in general. I think I could listen to you read a refrigerator manual."

I give a surprised laugh. "I think it would eventually put you to sleep."

"Maybe that's what I need to get to sleep tonight. Have a manual handy?"

"I don't, but I have a mystery novel by the bed," I say, reaching for the book. "I'll read you to sleep."

She laughs in response.

"I'm serious. I was going to read anyway."

I hear her yawn. "You don't need to do that."

"I don't mind."

"You might spoil me, and I'll never be able to fall asleep on my own again."

"I'm counting on it."

There's a pause, and I just know she's smiling, shaking her head. "Alright, read to me, Alex."

Alex. No one has called me Alex since secondary school. I love that she did. I hope she'll do it again.

"Are you settled in?" I ask.

"Mmm hmm."

Half an hour passes before my asking "are you awake" receives no response. My heart pounds as I end the call. What I'm feeling doesn't make sense. I've known this woman for less than a day. And logistically, the odds stack against us, but I can't help but be hopeful.

Before I try to sleep, I text Grey. I want to tell her about Ivy, because I know that Grey, ever the optimist, will pump me up even further.

——*ell*——

Late the next morning I wake and join Mrs. Brown in the kitchen. She has breakfast waiting (including baked beans) and asks me if I'm ever going to be up at a normal breakfast time. The answer is, who knows?

"How is your father?" I ask as I settle at the kitchen table. Mrs. Brown and I speak on the phone once a month when I'm in the US. During our last conversation she said her father was in the hospital recovering from an appendectomy.

"He's recovered well. Thank you for asking." She pats my arm as she bends to join me at the table. "What do you have planned for the day? Any riddles to solve?"

"I don't have anything planned until this afternoon. I'm meeting someone at Tower Bridge. That was the answer to my latest riddle."

"That seems odd given how personal the last one was."

"I'm going into this assuming there will be neither rhyme nor reason. But I'll keep you up to date."

We continue to chat as I finish my breakfast, then I swim some laps in the indoor pool. I smile at the children's toys sitting in a bin in the corner. The Browns must have had their grandchildren over for a swim. Good. I'm glad it's getting some use. If you ask me, this is the best part of the house. I wonder if Ivy and her family would want to come for a swim.

10

IVY

VAL HAS TO PULL me away from a food truck selling fish and chips as we walk into Jubilee Gardens to meet Alex. We did just have lunch, but the smell took me back to dinner last night. And last night's dinner was out of this world.

"Come on, we're already late," Val says.

I give her a look.

"What?" she asks.

"I'm still getting used to grown-up and responsible Val. Remember when you made us late for school, then when we got there you didn't have shoes on?"

Val laughs. "I've come a long way in the last decade and a half."

"You have." I put my arm around my sister's shoulders. "I'm

proud of you." And I am. Growing up with me as her mother, and our mother as an indifferent roommate didn't exactly set her up for success.

Val smiles as she brings her arm around my waist and squeezes. "Now where were we supposed to meet your new boyfriend, exactly?"

I roll my eyes. She has been calling Alex my boyfriend all morning, despite my protests. "He should be …" My eyes search and land on Alex. He's sitting on a bench behind a newspaper; still, I know it's him. His disguise, once again, is subpar. He has on another ball cap, this one navy blue with some design I can't make out from this distance. He looks up from the newspaper and catches my eye. He's wearing his glasses. I've always had a thing for glasses. He folds his paper and walks toward us, his t-shirt and jeans looking like they were tailor-made for him. Maybe they were?

"Hello." Alex aims a grin at me and then around at the rest of my family. "Planning to stick with your family today, Peter?" he asks with an especially large smile at my nephew.

Peter takes him seriously. "Yes, I do. They fussed at me for an hour about strangers and getting snatched."

I was there and it was fifteen minutes at the most.

"Glad to hear nobody is getting snatched today," Alex responds.

"Why do you want to go to the London Eye if you live here?

I bet you come all the time and you're tired of it," Juniper guesses.

"I was born here, but I don't actually live here, not often anyway. So it's been a long time since I've been on it. I think it was in the year 2000, just after it opened."

"Whoa. That was almost in the 1900s," Juniper says.

"That wasn't that long ago; all the adults here were born in the 1900s," Micah says with a laugh.

Juniper is flabbergasted and Peter has mentally left, watching a squirrel scamper toward a tree.

"Hey, Alex. What is that animal?" I ask, pointing to the squirrel before it disappears.

Alex sees it, then turns, giving a knowing smirk. "It's a sqwi-ruhl."

Juniper and Peter burst out laughing and they argue with Alex as we walk toward the Eye.

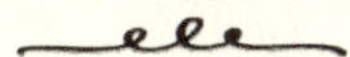

"It's a lot taller than the Ferris wheel at the fair." Juniper is backing away. It's nearly our turn to step into the bubble, or whatever you call it, we will ride around the eye.

"Ah, honey, it is," Micah says, "but it's entirely enclosed and look how well attached these things are to the circle."

He knows all the technical terms, like I do.

"Dad. What if a bolt shears off while we're at the top?"

Micah looks at his daughter and wife in confusion. "How?"

"We were looking at a broken lawn chair the other day and it had a rusty bolt that had been sheared off," Val says with a smile. "Juniper's smart."

"I'm smart too," Peter interjects.

"You definitely are," Val says.

"Something like this always has back-ups," Alex says to Juniper. "If one thing fails, there is something behind it to keep it from failing entirely. We'll be fine. Plus, I played a superhero in a movie once. So that's probably helpful, right?" he adds with a wink.

She eyes him up and down. "You'll hold my hand the whole time?"

"Absolutely. As long as you need me to." He holds out his hand and pulls it back as if reconsidering. "You don't have girl germs, do you? I hear sometimes girls have girl germs, and I don't know if I can risk it."

Juniper giggles, grabbing Alex's hand and pulling him to the bubble. "I don't have germs, SuperZander! Let's go!"

"Yeah, SuperZander, let's go." I eye him before turning to lead the group into our bubble. Why does Alex have to be so unbelievable?

11

ALEXANDER

JUNIPER'S HAND IS NOT the one I'd envisioned holding on this ride, not that it isn't nice in its own way. She's a sweet girl and I'm glad I can help her. Of course, my superhero skills will be useless if something happens. I know that. She knows that. But here we are. I'm a hundred percent sure I wouldn't be holding Ivy's hand right now, anyway. My right hand is free, but she has kept herself busy with Peter on the far side of our capsule.

"This goes way slower than a Ferris wheel," Juniper observes.

"It does. But we will only go around one time," I tell her.

"That stinks. I bet you go around on a Ferris wheel fifty times."

"Well, I believe it takes thirty minutes to go around this once. So we would be here for quite some time if we went around fifty times."

"Twenty-five hours. That's over a full day!"

She *is* a smart girl. I lean over toward her ear and whisper, "And there's no bathroom."

Juniper giggles and turns back toward the view. I feel Ivy's eyes on me and turn my head toward her with a smile. I'm stunned at how beautiful she is. The sun streaming into the capsule makes her skin glow and her hair shine with tiny stripes of gold. I have to get to know her. I have to shoot my shot with her before her vacation's over and she's gone.

"Will you point out all the best things to see from here?" Juniper asks.

"I'll be glad to. Obviously, there's Large Robert," I say, pointing toward Big Ben.

Juniper laughs. "Peter, come over here. Mr. Henry is about to give us the best tour."

"And highly accurate, don't forget highly accurate," I play-whisper to her.

Peter is followed by the rest of the family. "I already saw everything there is to see," he says, looking a little under-whelmed.

"Did you see Large Robert?" Juniper says with a raised eye-brow, making me laugh.

"Large Robert? What the heck are you talking about?" Peter looks skeptical.

Juniper points to Big Ben and giggles again. "Show us something else, Mr. Henry."

I wasn't prepared for a show, but if some sort of lunatic tour will make the kids laugh and possibly endear me to their aunt, then so be it.

"If you look past Large Robert, you'll see Buckingham Palace."

"That's where the King lives," Juniper provides.

"He actually lives in Clarence House," I tell her. "Buckingham Palace houses hundreds of male deer and thousands of pigs."

The kids look up at me in confusion. The joke has not landed with them, but the adults chuckle. I look up and meet Ivy's eyes, and they are the most open and interested I've seen them be, yet. I can't help the smile I send her way.

"Male deer are usually called bucks," Val tells her children. "And ham comes from pigs. *Buck*ing*ham* palace."

The kids are still unimpressed. Time to move on.

I continue touring them around London, trying to pepper in interesting facts with the humor, with varying degrees of success. It all has me feeling oddly nostalgic. For London, yes, but also, for doing things with a family. I didn't realize it was something I missed. My parents have been gone a while now, and before then, I wasn't around much. I'd left as quickly as I could. I had dreams and I was ready to pursue them.

Was this feeling a mix, though? Missing what I had and longing for it myself. I always assumed I'd have a family one day, but I've never pursued it. I certainly haven't made it a priority.

I'm staring out in the direction of my secondary school, remembering my first role, Ebenezer Scrooge in *A Christmas Carol*, when I'm hit with a realization. This is why my aunt has me on this wild goose chase. Not because she was crackers, though she was, but because she always hated that I left. She accused me of forgetting my roots, and trading in something established and beautiful for something frivolous and transient.

I don't agree, but as I look around, I have to admit, she wasn't entirely wrong.

I step to the side of the group and take a selfie with the view in the background, just in case this ends up being one of the stops Aunt Agnes has waiting for me.

"Are there not enough photos of yourself out there that you had to take a selfie?" Ivy smirks playfully as she approaches.

For a moment, I consider telling her about my aunt's mission, but it sounds insane and I'm not sure that having an insane aunt adds points in my favor.

"I just wanted to see how I really look in my new glasses," I joke.

"Have you not walked past a mirror since you got them?" Her eyes sparkle with mischief.

"Nope."

"A placid lake?"

This makes me chuckle and I imagine threading my fingers into her wild curls. "I only visit turbulent bodies of water," I say, stepping slightly closer.

Ivy tilts her head, considering. "Your glasses are perfect. In fact, I think I prefer you with them." She moves as if she were going to walk away. Like she wants to leave me to sit with that comment, which, judging from her facial expression, she meant as a compliment. No way I'm leaving a compliment unanswered. Not from her. I need to keep it light, though. She doesn't need to know that I could wax poetic about each and every one of her freckles. That the shape of her is the inspiration for love songs.

I stop her with the lightest drag of my knuckles down her cheek. "Your face is perfect. In fact, I think I prefer you with it."

Her laughter echoes around the capsule, and my heart soars with the sound.

12

IVY

"I was wrong when I said we were going to London Bridge. We're actually going to the Tower Bridge," I say as I look up from the itinerary on my phone. Yes, I made an itinerary. That's who I am.

"I know." Alex glances over the back seat of a fancy black car to where I sit. When Alex offered for his driver to drive the two of us to the bridge, my sister made a face that said *I'll never forgive you if you don't go.*

"You know? Are you all-knowing, too?"

"Too? What else am I?" he asks, the corner of his mouth turned up within his profile.

"You know good and well what all you are." He begs for my sassy attitude; he really does.

He shakes his head. "I knew you were going to the Tower Bridge because either you are like most tourists and assume Tower Bridge is London Bridge, or you know but misspoke. I'm guessing the latter, because you don't strike me as the type to go into a trip without some research."

I turn my phone face down so he can't see my detailed spreadsheet. He's got me pegged there, but there's no need for him to see how right he actually is.

—ℓℓ—

We step into the north tower and are greeted by a spiral staircase. I've always wanted a house with a spiral staircase, but this one looks daunting.

"Construction began in 1886 and took eight years to complete," I read off a sign. "That's amazing. I wonder if they've had to replace much of it."

"My grandma still uses a blender she got for her wedding. Things used to be built to last," Micah supplies.

"What he left out is that her blender was also built in 1886," Val jokes from the step two above mine. The kids lead the way, followed by Micah, and Alex is bringing up the rear. I'm trying *not* to think about *my* rear, being right in his face. Still, I'm glad I wore my best jeans today. I'm sure I can't match the near physical perfection he's used to in women, but I feel good in these jeans. Not that I'm thinking about it.

Okay, I totally am. But how could I not be with almost everyone's "ideal man" right behind me?

We make it up to the pedestrian bridge and my eyes go straight for the floor, which is over half covered in glass. You can see straight through it to the bridge surface below. Will I be walking over the glass surface? Absolutely not. I will skirt the edge and not look down.

I ignore the catch in my throat when the kids start walking, then jumping, *jumping*, on top of the glass. Eyes straight forward and focused on the exit to the stairs at the other end. In my research, I'd seen the glass floor, but I hadn't anticipated reacting like this. I was fine in the Eye, but there's something about a glass floor that has my brain saying, "It's too risky!"

I take a deep breath.

"Are you alright?" Alex leans in to whisper. "Is the floor looking a bit dodgy to you?"

Typically, I'd feel embarrassed, but something about Alex doesn't allow that. Before I know what's happening, he has taken my hand and is hurrying us along.

"Want me to distract you?

Just him asking distracts me. What is even going on with this man right now? And why is he looking at me like I'm his entire focus?

"How would you distract me?"

"I could sing a song."

From the corner of my eye, I see a teenage girl taking a photo of us. She'll likely Photoshop her face onto me and then tape the picture to her wall.

"I think you draw enough attention without singing. I didn't even know you could sing. Not that I know everything about you," I add, not wanting him to think I went back to the hotel and googled him after we had ice cream. Of course I did, but I didn't take a super deep dive. I'm not a weirdo.

"Oh, I don't really sing. Or rather, I do, but only in the shower or in the car."

"In that case, I think that's exactly what I need to take my mind off the dodgy glass floor."

Alex laughs at my dodgy use of dodgy and begins belting out that famous song from the musical *Annie*. He's in the middle of the word tomorrow when my hand clamps down over his mouth.

"That sort of thing is illegal in enclosed spaces." I pull him toward the exit, my eyes catching on my sister's smirking expression as I look back to make sure they know we are leaving. Of course they already know. He made a spectacle, and now my sister is mentally planning our wedding.

We've walked away from the bridge, and I'm not exactly sure where we're going until Alex turns and says, "This is a great view of the bridge. I didn't want you to miss it. Great for photos."

He's right. I hand him my phone. "Family photo time! Come on, kids."

We line up in front of the bridge and Alex, with the flair of a Hollywood director, takes a few shots. He hands my phone back and I find he took a selfie while he waited for us to get ready. It's a ridiculous photo, but he looks so good. I've had a thing for dark hair and blue eyes since I was a preteen and saw *Frodo* on the cover of a magazine at a grocery store.

No offence to Elijah Wood, but Alex standing here making small talk with my brother-in-law beats grocery store *Frodo* any day.

I slide my phone back into my pocket as Alex steps back to me.

"Micah's going to take a photo of us."

"You want to take a photo with me?"

"Of course. I'd be a fool not to, and I need a photo of myself with the bridge. I'll tell you about that in a minute," he adds when I give him a questioning look.

We turn and he puts his arm around my shoulders, snuggling me into his side and I don't hate it. It feels so good here and I've been missing something like this for years without realizing it. Would it feel this good with someone else? I mean, probably. But maybe not.

I tilt my head toward Alex and smile while Micah takes exactly one photo. Alex should have asked Val to do it.

"It's really good," Alex says, handing me his phone. He's right. It's the most stunning photo of myself I have ever seen. I think maybe it's my proximity to Alex, but still, I can't help my smile. I'm not usually terribly photogenic, so this is a novel sight.

"I'll send it to you," he says when I hand him back the phone.

"Thanks. Want to tell me about why you *needed* a photo of yourself by the Tower Bridge?"

Val and Micah watch the kids play on the steps of the amphitheater we're standing near, as Alex tells me about his aunt and her crazy stipulations on his grandfather's box. I can't believe her lawyer let her set this up.

"I've never heard of anything like this happening," I comment.

"My aunt was a bit out there." Alex pushes his glasses up the bridge of his nose.

"I bet she was fun to have around."

"Sometimes ..." He looks out to the water, then to me. "I talked to Grey and my agent, and we're calling things off. Saying we broke up after the movie premiere."

"Why?" For me? Surely not.

"I didn't feel comfortable pursuing anything with"—he eyes me—"anyone else, while supposedly together with her. I wouldn't want to turn the other woman into the *other woman*."

"So you didn't do this for me in particular?"

"I definitely did it for you in particular." He reaches out and runs his hand down the back of mine. I stare back at him for a beat.

"Anizey! Come play London Bridge with us!"

"Duty calls." I smile, relieved not to have to respond, and run off to join the kids. I'm flattered, but I don't truly know how to feel that he would do that for me. Holy cow.

13

ALEXANDER

I WATCH AS IVY squats to walk underneath the kid's joined hands. Their uninhibited singing of *London Bridge*, in front of the Tower Bridge, makes me smile. Their game unwittingly turning into a performance. And Ivy is a performer. Not in the heading to Broadway sort of way, but she's graceful and beautiful in her movements, and her smile is more captivating than I've seen it.

"Mr. Henry, come play! We need someone else to lock up!" Their parents have both declined, so I, the last resort, head their way.

"Good luck if you get locked up," Ivy loudly whispers to me. "These jailers are rough."

"I can take it," I answer with a confident smile.

"We can be extra rough with him," I hear Peter whisper to Juniper.

I'm, of course, locked up when it comes to that part of the song, and they are indeed rough. I narrowly miss a hit to the eggs. Ivy finds it all endlessly funny, and if I'm not mistaken, there's affection in her eyes. It could be entirely for her niece and nephew, but something tells me it isn't.

I'm released and feeling pretty good about life. "Do you all have dinner plans? I'd love to take you all somewhere if you don't."

"We don't," Val quickly answers. The look Ivy gives her tells me they likely *did* have plans. Or at least an idea. But I'm not deterred.

"Brilliant! We'll call a second car," I offer.

We're walking toward the front of the restaurant when Ivy leans into me and whispers. "Do children eat here?"

"Yes."

"Are you sure? Because this looks very fancy. *And* we are not dressed for fancy."

"We'll have our own room. No one will even see us."

"How? When did you arrange that? I've been with you since you mentioned dinner."

"I texted my assistant when we were walking to the car."

"Ah. I thought you were sending the photo of us to the solicitor." She bobbles her head hastily and says *solicitor* in an English accent, and I don't know that she could be any more endearing. Huh. Crescent's fake accent drove me up the wall. I guess it was because it was her.

"I sent it to him when I sent it to you. Speaking of, have you made the photo your lock screen yet?"

"Ha. Have you? And also, you have an assistant who arranges for private dining. Man, you live in another world."

I pull out my phone and change my lock screen, then turn it to Ivy. "There. Now I'll smile every time I pick up my phone."

She rolls her eyes and smiles. "I'm not changing mine, Casanova." She shows her screen to me, and the photo is one of her, Juniper, and Peter clearly taken years ago. "This is prime real estate."

I pocket my phone and open the door for Ivy and her family. As she walks past me, I catch her scent briefly, and it's as if she's tied a string to me and is pulling me behind her. There is something about the way her delicate floral scent mixes with her natural smell that attracts me like a moth to a raging bonfire.

"Mr. Henry. Welcome. Right this way." A host smiles as he approaches us from behind a podium. "Carlo will be your dedicated server," he says as he leads us into a dimly lit room.

"Thank you," I say with a nod, then make my way to the table where I pull out a chair for Ivy. She suppresses a smile as she thanks me and sits. I sit to her left, across from Juniper.

"Does this place have chicken tenders?" Juniper asks.

"I don't know," I answer. "But I'm sure there will be something you'll like."

"You have more faith in that than you should," Val says. "She is pickier than Peter, and trust me, that's saying a lot."

"Hello, my name is Carlo, and it will be my pleasure to serve you this evening." Carlo moves around the table taking drink orders before disappearing.

"This place serves tapas, so I took the liberty to have them bring us a selection of their most popular dishes to share, along with some options for the children. Hopefully, there will be something satisfactory for all." Then something dawns on me. "Does anyone have food allergies? I didn't think about that."

"We're all good," Ivy answers, and I can tell she's pleased by this situation. I wonder if, being a restaurateur, she loves trying new foods. Or maybe she is the type to love surprises. I'd love to surprise her. Often.

As it turns out, this family is very vocal when it comes to the enjoyment of their food. From the adults, a chorus of moans, groans, and favorable adjectives. From the kids, there are also groans, but theirs are something more akin to fervent detestation. As it turns out, this particular fancy restaurant does *not* cater to the picky child.

"I'm hungry," Peter says as he stares down at the grilled chicken and candied sweet potatoes on his plate.

"You know, sometimes I just love a simple toast with peanut butter and jam."

"I love peanut butter and jelly. Is that the same?" Juniper asks.

"Essentially, yes. And my housekeeper makes the best bread."

"What's a housekeeper?" Peter asks, at the same time as Juniper asks, "Can we go to your house and have a sandwich?"

I look up to their parents and Ivy, because as much as I would love to have them all over, I don't want to agree to something that isn't okay. I nod to the adults, giving my assent.

"Yes, we can go for a sandwich," Micah says. "Hand me your plate, Peter. I want to try those sweet potatoes."

The kids cheer, and Ivy smiles, bumping me with her shoulder. "Will there be a lady's maid who can attend to me?" she whispers.

"I can arrange for one," I say, pulling out my phone. She laughs, and I open my texts.

ALEX

Do you all have swimsuits? I have a pool.

"I think I heard your phone buzz."

Ivy gives me a quizzical look, then pulls her phone from her pocket.

BEAUTIFUL IVY

> We do. But I'm pretty sure I hear rain.

ALEX

> It's indoors. Check with the others. I'd love to have you all for swimming. We can stop by your hotel for your things.

ALEX

> Or just you. If you need some alone time with me.

I see her smile and shake her head, drawing Val's attention. "Are y'all textin' while you're sittin' together?"

Ivy simply smiles at her sister.

BEAUTIFUL IVY

> I'll check with them.

14

IVY

ALEXANDER'S HOME IS LIKE every dream I've ever had when thinking I'd like to renovate a house one day. Although, I get the feeling this kind of character could never be replicated in a home built after 1950, my jaw had dropped when he told us it was built in the early 1800s.

There are marble floors, stunning hardwoods, and the most beautiful rugs you can imagine. There is some kind of plaster embossing in various areas of the walls, bringing a charm that makes me drool. The huge stone fireplaces and beautifully detailed doorways beg to be photographed. I never realized how high class I am. Excuse me while I pass out.

The most mind-blowing thing of all is ... to Alex this is normal. He grew up here. He has no idea how normal people live. I mean, I don't know how he could. Maybe he has done something to try to relate with the gutter rats in the rest of society. Maybe when he moved to America, he only took the clothes on his back and a smile. A gorgeous smile, which most people would say he'd needed to leave at home as well if he were truly trying to see how the world works for the average person.

He could be a world-class snob, and I'd hardly be able to fault him for it, but he hasn't come across that way in the least.

A woman meets us in the kitchen—a utilitarian, but still beautiful, space. She is perhaps in her late fifties or early sixties, with beautiful silver hair put up in a perfect messy bun. I love the look.

"Oh. Alexander, and you've brought guests! Hello!"

Alex introduces everyone, and a chorus of greetings meets her. It takes about thirty seconds for Mrs. Brown to completely charm us all. There's just something about her. I don't know if it's her accent or her grandmotherly ways, or likely both. The kids don't really have any grandparents in their lives. Micah's parents live in Oregon, and, of course, our mom isn't a grandmother, like she was never a real mother.

Mrs. Brown takes the kids to the pantry to choose a snack to have with their sandwich. I get the feeling she could steal the children away, and everyone involved—children included—would shrug and assume it was for the best.

Rain is softly hitting the glass roof of the indoor pool. It, like the rest of the house, doesn't disappoint. Glass arches above us, and exotic-looking plants line the walls. The space had obviously been updated to keep up with pool technology, but it was done in a way that didn't interrupt the historic charm.

I want to be put off by the fact that there are people who live like this, but I'm not. And watching Alex humbly answering Micah's questions about the place does nothing to aid in that.

Alex drops a stack of pale green towels on a table and pulls off his shirt. It's nothing that I, and the whole world, haven't seen before, but in person? In person he's a whole other thing. My eyes are trying to figure out where to start with all the dips and ridges, when he catches my gaze, a playful smirk lighting his face.

"You seem to be enjoying yourself," he says as he approaches me.

"It's lovely in here. Do you tend to all the plants?"

He laughs. "Yes, I fly in each time they need watering." He pauses and looks around the space. "My mum was the master gardener. She loved her garden in the warm months, but wanted more when it was cold out. I remember when they were small. They looked silly in this huge room, but now ... she would have been so pleased with how they look."

I smile softly, wondering at how he feels. Mom was lost to us ages ago, really we never had her, but I imagine losing Val and I think maybe I can understand.

"How long has she been gone?"

"Two years this coming September. Lost them both in a car crash." Alex pushes his glasses up the bridge of his nose.

"Oh my gosh. How awful." I rub my hand along his upper arm and refuse to feel his muscle there. Now isn't the time. "I'm so sorry."

"It was certainly awful, but I'm alright now." He smiles at the sound of Peter yelling and jumping in the pool. "Anyway, I didn't mean to bring down the mood. Let's swim."

He turns and walks toward the pool while I pull off the t-shirt I'd been using as a coverup. His eyes are on me as I walk to the stairs, and he looks like a man entranced. I wouldn't consider my vintage-cut, coral-and-white striped swimsuit terribly sexy, but given Alex's face, he would disagree.

I sigh as I step into the water. What is even happening right now?

"Hey, Mr. Henry! Will you score me when I jump in?" Peter calls from across the pool.

"Sure. Am I scoring for style?"

"I guess so. Rate it from one to ten."

I float around the pool—the forgotten cool aunt—as Alex rates both the kids as they do various jumps and dives into the water. The man has endless patience. I would have encouraged them to do something else after ten or so jumps.

"Well, he's good with kids." Val surprises me, whispering over my shoulder.

"Yes. He's made that abundantly clear all day."

"Hmm. He also made it abundantly clear that he wants to—"

"Yeah, yeah." I interrupt, looking over my shoulder at my grinning sister, who shrugs and swims off. I certainly don't need her telling me what I already know. This man is sucking me into his vortex fast.

Movement draws my eye to the water in front of me. I expected it to be one of the kids; instead, it's Alex. He pops up, dripping water just like he did in that movie. What was it called? I don't think my brain's working.

He stands close. I look over his shoulder and find my family engrossed in a game of Marco Polo. The back of his hand grazes mine, and my eyes find his again.

"Hey, you," he says, looking at me with wonder. Or maybe surprise.

"Hello." I swallow as his eyes bore into mine. The intensity makes me uncomfortable, so I search my brain for something, anything, to say. "You have an excellent house."

He laughs, tangling his fingers with mine. Not holding them … more like … playing with them. The simple sensation threatens to melt me right into the water of this pool.

"You made that clear earlier when you couldn't keep your mouth from hanging open."

I cover my mouth with my hand and feel the tiniest amount of heat filling my cheeks. He steps slightly closer and slowly pulls my hand down. "No need to be embarrassed. I'm a big fan of your mouth, and it gave me another reason to look."

When I didn't, couldn't, respond, he continues in hushed tones. "Would you like me to tell you the other reasons I like your mouth?"

"I got you!" Peter screams as he and Micah crash near us, bringing me back to the reality of where we are and who we're with.

"I'm gonna go to the bathroom," I say in a panic.

When I come out of the bathroom a couple of minutes later, Alex is standing in the hallway looking as handsome as ever, but shockingly sheepish.

"I'm sorry I followed you. I ... I just ..." He cuts the distance between us in half. "I don't know. There's just something about you that makes me feel the need to be near you." He comes to stand right in front of me, almost trapping me between himself and the wall. "I don't know what it is, and I certainly can't explain the insanity of feeling like this after knowing you for two days, but I ... you ..." He smooths a damp curl out of my face, sending my pulse skyrocketing. "You have the most beautiful hair." His sheepishness is gone as he gently slides his hand down my jaw to cup my chin, slowly bringing his thumb to my lower lip and torturously moving along its surface. Once again, my brain refuses to work. "I mentioned I'm a big fan of your mouth." My breaths stutter as he erases the space between us and sets his cheek against mine, then whispers, "You have the most perfect pink lips, and I'm always finding myself on the edge of my seat waiting for what you'll say next. That's why I love your mouth, in case you were wondering."

Then he steps back and walks toward the pool, leaving me in a puddle behind him.

The man shocks me at every turn. Less than forty-eight hours with him has made me want to have eight black-haired, blue-eyed babies with accent confusion. Ideally, they would have his accent, but if we lived in North Carolina, that wouldn't last. We could visit England frequently, but that would cost a fortune. Not that that would matter, I guess. Good grief. No. I'm not looking for complicated. I'm looking for someone who simplifies things. Not for someone who would absolutely turn things upside down. Right now, I'm tilting, but need to bring myself upright again.

15

Alexander

THERE'S A STRANGE SILENCE in the car. Despite the relatively short ride from my house to the hotel, I think the kids may be asleep. Val and Micah aren't talking. Maybe they're tired too, or maybe they're giving Ivy and me space to talk. But we aren't and I'm stressed.

Did I scare her by coming on too strong? I wanted to kiss her. It might have been too soon, but the way she reacted to me—her ragged breathing and the way she looked at me—told me maybe it wouldn't have been. I'd planned to ask her to join me for some of the things with my aunt's riddles, but would she want to? I think she's got into her head thinking about logistics. I mean, of course, it wouldn't be easy. We would have some things to figure out, but it would be worth it. Or it could be. And now *I'm* in *my* head. I met this woman yesterday and I'm considering the possibility of a huge life change for her.

I don't really know her. Still, something inside me wants to keep trying, and see where things go.

"Would you sit here with me for a minute?" I ask as I pull up in front of the hotel.

"Sure," she says. I tell her family goodnight and she promises to be up shortly, and then we're alone.

"Thank you for everything," she says. "For showing us your home and letting us swim. Oh, and for dinner, it was really good."

"Next time we'll go somewhere that has food the kids will like."

"Next time? I ... I'm not so sure there should be a next time. Why would we—"

"Because I would love to see more of you. Get to know you."

"To what end?" Ivy asks. "I want to be honest. I'm not a fling person. I also don't live in California or England. I'm certainly not looking for a transcontinental relationship."

"I don't live here. It would just be across the country at first."

She sighs. "You've been incredible to me. To my family. And I genuinely like you. But I think the Venn diagram of our lives is only going to overlap on this trip. I love my life and I have to believe there is someone out there who would easily fit into it. Nothing would be simple with us. I don't want to become attached to you only for things to get too hard, and I really don't want you to come into my life only to be halfway there. I've had enough of that in my life already and I'm not going to allow it to happen again."

"I could—"

"Do you really want to upend your life for a woman you met yesterday? If we don't get to know each other further, we can avoid a lot of heartache."

"You don't think it could be worth trying?"

"I don't want to try for something that's impossible." Ivy opens her door slightly. "You'll find someone who fits your life and I'll find someone who fits mine. We'll be happy; it just won't be together."

She leans over and kisses my cheek. I close my eyes, concentrating on the feel of it, rather than what's happening inside me. I open my eyes at the sound of her door closing and watch as she walks inside, not looking back.

I come into my house to the smell of biscuits baking. It's unlike Mrs. Brown to cook at night. Generally, once she cleans up dinner, she closes down the kitchen for the night. I follow the smell and the sound of her tuneless humming.

"I'm making biscuits so the next time you bring them here

I'll have some for the kids. I'll pull them out of the freezer if you give me a heads-up. They will be around several more days, right?"

"I don't think they'll be back," I say, taking a biscuit from the cooling rack. Shortbread with chocolate chips and walnuts. Mrs. Brown always remembers my favorites. I smile, feeling a bit lighter.

"Why not? They were delightful. And that Ivy; I saw how you looked at her. And how she looked at you. What happened?"

"Logistics happened." I shrug, portraying an indifference I'm not feeling. "She thinks there's too much we would have to overcome, and we'd just end up with heartbreak in the end."

Mrs. Brown drops her oven glove on the counter. "And what do you think?"

I sigh. "I'm not sure she's wrong."

"You like her a lot, don't you?"

I pick up a second biscuit. "I think so. But how could I? I've known her for two days. That's not really long enough to know. She could have some monstrous habits I've yet to see. What if she enjoys kicking the canes out from under old people?" I try to make light of the situation, but it falls flat. For Mrs. Brown and for me.

"I'm sorry, lad." She pats me on the arm. "Give it a day or two and see how you feel."

I nod and watch as she puts three more biscuits on a plate for me and checks the last pan in the oven, then take my plate to the living room.

I sit in my mum's favorite place, a sage green tufted armchair, and pull out my phone. I'm met with the photo I'd jokingly put as my lock screen. We look like a couple in love. We hold each other like we've done it hundreds of times. And I want to. I'm not sure I've ever wanted anything more.

I open my photos to one I took when Ivy wasn't looking. She's looking out toward the Tower Bridge. I'd looked over at her, and the lighting was perfect. She looked perfect. I sigh and send the photo to her, without words.

16

IVY

I'D CUT OFF MY phone when I got inside the hotel last night. I didn't want to risk hearing from him or going down the rabbit hole that is the Alexander Henry corner of the internet. Now I sit on the sofa in our room, eating the breakfast pastry Micah brought me and staring down at the photo Alex sent me last night.

"You look gorgeous!" Val says as she looks over my shoulder. I haven't told my sister about my conversation with Alex. I don't want her opinion on it. At least not yet. When I don't respond, she continues, "I wanna see the one of y'all together."

I'd been tempted to delete it, but I didn't. I couldn't. I open the photo and pass the phone to Val.

"Wow. You guys look perfect together. Like ... oh, are you

going to post this on your socials? You should!"

"No. Definitely not."

"Why? Oh, wait. He has a girlfriend! I totally forgot. He doesn't act like he has a girlfriend." She looks incredibly disappointed. "He seems like such a good person."

"Their relationship wasn't real. Their agents set it up. You can't tell anyone."

"What? It looks so real." Val hands me back my phone.

"They're actors," I say with a shrug.

"That's a valid point. And really, sis, now I'm wondering if you could ever trust him. He could lie to you so easily. But at the same time, he seems so genuine and good. I don't feel like he would." Her face was thoughtful as she collapsed on the sofa beside me.

"I don't either." I look back at our picture. "Wait. You said their relationship *wasn't* real."

"Oh yeah. He ended it."

"FOR YOU?" Val jumps off the sofa, and stares down at me in shock.

"Yep."

"Oh, girl. This is your chance."

"But I barely know him."

"You've got the chance to get to know him."

No. As much as I might want to, I'm not going to.

We go to Greenwich Market to shop and have lunch. It's a mix of vendor stands and brick-and-mortar stores. I've seen glass art, prints of paintings, handmade clothes, and a booth containing truly intriguing flavors of hot sauce. We have snacked our way around the place. Mine and Micah's favorite was the Coxinha. It was served to us by a tiny Brazilian woman. The chicken, cheese and spices were battered and fried. Peter said they looked like dinosaur tears, and they did. I mean, if a dinosaur were to cry.

I'm standing waiting on Val to finish her Chinese dumplings when an ice cream stand catches my eye and makes me think of Alex. Until then, I'd done a surprisingly good job of keeping my mind off him as we shopped, but it's the waffle cones that take me back to him.

I feel good about my decision, but does that mean I can't miss him? No. But I definitely don't *want* to think about what might have been. I've made my choice and it's for the best.

Still, I wonder what he's up to today. Has he gotten another one of his aunt's crazy riddles? I wish I wasn't so curious about what's in his grandfather's box. Is it mementos? Is it gold bars? Is it empty with only a note that says "Sucker!"?

Would it be too inappropriate for me to ask him to let me know? Probably.

"You want my last dumpling?" Val asks, handing me her tray, already knowing I'd want it.

"Thanks." I pop the bite in and wish I wasn't already stuffed. I'd go get more if I had a place to put them.

We continue walking through the outdoor part of the market until a light sprinkle of rain turns into a downpour, forcing us—and everyone around us—into the nearest store: a shop containing antiques and collectables, and about twenty too many people for the small space.

I stand pressed up against the window with Val and Juniper. The boys were pushed to another part of the store.

"This stinks," Juniper says as she attempts to step further from an older woman's giant pocketbook.

"It surely won't last long," Val says.

"We can find something in here to distract ourselves," I suggest. I look around and only see people crammed together. My eyes don't land on a single item for sale that we can talk about. "Maybe there's something outside?"

We all turn to look out the window, and there isn't much to see. Through the curtain of rain, I can see quite a few people huddled under the awning in front of a jewelry store.

"There's Alexander!" Juniper says in a near yell as she points through the rain toward the people.

"What?" There's no way he's here, huddled under an awning with strangers.

"Where?" Val asks.

"Look on the right, underneath the W. He's wearing jeans, a black t-shirt, and a white hat," Juniper supplied.

Val gasped at the same time my eyes landed on him. I'm not convinced; the rain's heavy and the man is looking down. It sure looks like him, though, which is a big compliment to the man if he's *not* Alex.

"You should go see him. How romantic would that be for you to run through the rain to get to him?"

"It would be romantic if it's him. If it's not, I'll just anger the crowd already squeezed too tightly together for no reason."

"Do it, Anizey! I like him."

"Me too." Val grins.

I shake my head, not believing I'm actually considering heading over there. I look out toward the man again. The rain has let up a bit, and the man still looks like Alex. I know what I told him, and nothing has changed, but the urge to run over even for the chance to see him is strong. It's like I feel as if I've been given one more chance to see him, and maybe I shouldn't waste it.

"Alright, I'll go."

Juniper starts jumping up and down, knocking the woman's pocketbook off her shoulder. "Sorry!"

The woman smiles at Juniper and readjusts her bag.

"Really?" Val asks, like this is the most shocking news she

has ever received.

"What do I have to lose?"

"Your dry shirt," Juniper supplies.

"I'll move fast."

I make my way arduously through the crowd and out the door, then run across the bricks, only coming to a stop when I'm at the feet of the man. I look up to meet the beautiful brown eyes of a stranger.

This is what I get for being impulsive and diverting from what I know is right. A wet shirt and the confused gaze of the second most handsome man in England.

17

ALEXANDER

I'M SITTING UP ON the weight bench in the gym by the indoor pool and find myself on my phone. Once again, I'm staring at the photo of me and Ivy. Am I crazy? Is it absolutely bonkers that I'm acting like she's the love of my life who ended things with me after a five-year relationship? If someone I knew were in my situation, I'd probably say ... suck it up. You've known her for two days, you idiot.

Except I'm the idiot.

I've always been a little impulsive. The type to jump in with both feet. Filled with enthusiasm and optimism. You should have heard the talks my father had with me before I left for California. But there was no stopping me from going to Hollywood, writing, directing and maybe acting some. I was all in.

Excited to pursue my dream.

That was years ago, and I like to think I've gained some wisdom and life experience since then, but it seems I reverted to my old ways—at least where Ivy's concerned. It's like I saw her and parts of my now fully formed brain simply turned off. She was right. Of course she was right, but there I was on the edge of the cliff with my shoes off, ready to jump into that water, no matter how far below me it was.

She probably thought I was a naïve fool.

Ivy is smart and successful and has worked hard to achieve her goals. I have had to work hard very little in my life. While I wouldn't say I was born with a silver spoon in my mouth, I had plenty of opportunities handed to me. There was always money and connections growing up. And once I moved to Hollywood, my looks got me in places which would take a more average-looking person years to get into. That makes me sound like a snob, but I know what I look like, and I certainly noticed when doors easily opened which should have remained closed. Thankfully, I had a natural talent to go along with my looks that kept me in the business.

Not that that's impressive to Ivy. It makes me smile, remembering her initial reaction to me. I loved it. I *am* just a person; I just so happen to be in the public eye. The concept of celebrity is weird to me, especially now that I'm there. I don't actually want to be famous. I want to create and live my life in peace.

I force myself to pocket my phone and lie back down on the weight bench. I'd thought a punishing workout would take my mind off Ivy. It hasn't, but I'm not going to quit.

***

I make a protein smoothie with cherries and walnuts, then sit at the table in the kitchen. Of course, I pull out my phone. This time, I bypass the photo and search her name online.

There isn't a lot. There's a story on her local news site about the fire that destroyed her restaurant, Bowl. It looks like it had been a very popular spot in a fairly small town. I wonder how many restaurants they have there. Probably not many, judging by the virtual walk I'm taking down Main Street.

Then I go to Bowl's website. There's a page with Ivy's picture and a short bio. She has an MBA and she's a self-taught cook. She loves the beach but is thankful to live near the mountains. It's not a lot to learn, but I'm glad to know it.

I move on to the menu. All the breakfast offerings remind me a little of the Parker's restaurant back in Thousand Oaks. I should send them a postcard; they'd get a kick out of that.

Bowl has many exciting dishes on the menu, but I plan to try the grits. That's something I've never tried, and I want to try Ivy's grits one day. I will when I go. If I go.

I'm sliding my phone back into my pocket when I feel it vibrate. It's my next riddle from Mr. Crawley.

It's a residence, but so much more
You can't just walk on through the door
A guard will stop you there
With a stiff and sombre stare

She really could have tried harder with that one. Buckingham Palace.

I wish Ivy were going with me.

18

IVY

"Do you think the King's in there right now?" Peter asks as we all stand near the Queen Victoria Memorial, looking at Buckingham Palace.

"I think there's a specific flag that flies up there if he is. We'll have to look it up," I answer. I try to run my fingers through my curls, but they are a tangled mess. The humidity today has them beyond their normal out-of-control nature. When I'm at home, I have products to combat the North Carolina humidity, but I didn't bring my entire arsenal.

Who cares? I'm not trying to impress anyone.

"Hey, look!" Juniper calls out. "Those girls are doing a dance in front of those guards, and the guards aren't even smiling!"

I think I could be a guard here. They wouldn't make me

smile either, even if I liked it. I watch one girl start twerking. Nevermind. I would have negative reactions all the time. I wonder if whoever is in charge monitors for eye rolls. I'd be fired on day one.

"I wish we'd been able to schedule a tour," Val says. "I think the kids would have liked it."

"A tour of a huge old house? Pass," Peter says, like he doesn't realize he's talking about one of the most famous *houses* in the world. And it's a palace. Come on, Peter.

I line my family up in front of the palace and take their picture. I see a notification of an email from my contractor. I read it, then collapse on the nearby steps.

He is estimating an additional month for repairs and fifteen thousand more dollars. I'm not terribly shocked about the money—there were things I wanted to upgrade while we were doing this—but seeing it spelled out, is staggering on top of losing another month's worth of income.

Ugh. I want comfort food.

"Can we eat at that place we ate on our first night? The one with the fish and chips?" I ask Val, who has walked over, looking concerned.

"Sure, as far as I'm concerned. I wanted to try everything on that menu. And I'm sure Micah doesn't care. *Food is just fuel.* Weirdo."

I smile absently as Val sits on the step beside me.

"Are you alright?" she asks.

I stretch my feet out in front of me. "I just got an email from my contractor. It's going to be more expensive and take longer than anticipated."

"I'm sorry, that stinks. You just now got that email? You've been in a funk all day."

I sigh. I guess I'll tell her. She'll start to wonder eventually anyway. "I told Alex it wouldn't work, and I didn't see any reason to keep seeing each other while we're here. It would just end in heartbreak."

My sister is silent for a moment, looking down at her shoes, before she turns to look over at me. "This is just like you. It's not simple. You don't feel like you can trust it, or make sure it fits into what you see for your life or your future, so you don't give it a chance."

"Not simple? I started a business. Do you think that was simple?"

"No, of course not. But you had everything planned to the letter. You made it fit into the mold for your life."

"Or did I change the *mold for my life* to include the restaurant?" I stand, frustrated. And, honestly, I don't know if I'm more frustrated with Val for being partially right, or with myself. I'm inflexible and untrusting. Those don't sound like positive characteristics, but until now they've served me well. Who's to say they aren't still? "I can change for the things that seem worth it. I can weigh the cost versus the benefit."

"And somehow you've already deemed Alex lacking in benefit?" She looks at me, shaking her head, then stands. "You're never—"

"I'm a realist. It's an impossible situation where one or both of us would have to give up the life we love. I don't want to do that, and I wouldn't ask that of him." I'm breathing hard. This is similar to arguments we've had before, but this time it's hitting me a little harder. "And I certainly don't want someone who will be in my life part-time. We've had enough of that."

She nods slowly. "Do you know that he loves his life?" Val says, her voice soft as she takes my hand. "What if he doesn't, and you miss something that would have been amazing?"

I have to believe amazing is waiting for me back in North Carolina, and this with Alex will become a crazy story I tell. *Some* people are impressed by actors. Not me, obviously.

Well, I might be impressed by this one, but it has nothing to do with his profession.

19

Alexander

I WAKE WITH A sense of sadness or desperation, like I came out of a dream which was particularly good. Maybe I did, but my mind won't take me back to check. I only feel the loss of it in my grogginess. As I awaken further, I'm reminded of another loss, and I wonder if that was the only one. Maybe my brain won't take me back to a dream because there wasn't one. Only the loss of a woman who was never even mine.

I get out of bed and open the curtains, the sun high in the sky. I'll get this sleep schedule sorted out by the time I head back to the States.

My phone pings with a notification. I hope it's Ivy, but it isn't.

GRAY

> Hey! I need an update on the Ivy situation. You guys in love yet?

ALEXANDER

> It's already over. She couldn't see past our logistical problems.

GRAY

> What? How? You're amazing! You're not giving up, are you?

ALEXANDER

> Yeah. I don't have a choice.

GRAY

> Is she still in London? If so, you need to give it one more shot. I'll be super mad at you if you don't.

I roll my eyes, but maybe she's right. I decide to text Ivy.

ALEXANDER

> Are you busy? Would you meet me somewhere? It can be as brief as you like.

It's not until I've showered and had breakfast that I hear back from her.

BEAUTIFUL IVY

> Sure. Val and Micah took the kids to do some kid things. I decided to hang back and find other things to get up to. Just tell me when and where.

Oh my gosh. She said she'll meet with me. I didn't even have to convince her. I hadn't let my hopes get too high, but now they are soaring.

———ell———

I'm sitting on a bench in a park near Ivy's hotel. I'd offered to pick her up, but she wanted to walk to meet me. Fair enough. It gave me time to stop and pick up a Cornish pasty. I hope she hasn't already tried one.

I'm holding the same newspaper from the other day in front of my face when someone who smells faintly of flowers sits beside me.

"Aren't you that famous actor? Brad Hawthorne? I almost didn't recognize you with this masterful disguise. Glasses *and* a newspaper? You really know what you're doing."

I smile toward my paper. She isn't shutting me out. This is a good sign. I turn my smile toward her. "You can't be too careful with the riff-raff around here." I eye her suspiciously. She's so beautiful. She's wearing a red dress with sneakers, and her hair is wilder than I've seen it. I love it, but the urge to touch it threatens to make this more awkward than it needs to be.

"I brought you something."

She narrows her eyes playfully at me. "You're not trying to buy me, are you, Mr. Hawthorne?"

"Oh. I know better than that. What did you say your name was again? Betty Copperfield?"

She snorts a laugh, and I'm delighted. She's in the mood to have some fun, and it will work right along with what I'm about to propose.

"Yes, I'm Betty, and I'm so curious about what you have for me, a person you just met on this bench."

I grin at her. Her fun side is really out to play today.

I grab the white paper bag that has been sitting to my right and hand it to Ivy. She looks excited as she opens the bag and pulls out the wrapped pasty.

"What is it?"

"It's a Cornish pasty. It has beef, vegetables, and seasonings. Have you already tried one?"

"No. This will be the first."

"Good. I thought, as a restaurateur, you might like to try something new. I noticed how you enjoyed trying the different foods at the restaurant the other night."

"I do love trying new foods. I also have problems hyper-fixating on foods, which keeps me from trying new things. You never know with me." She shrugs and pulls back the paper and took a bite and groaned. I simply watched as she closed her eyes, enjoying the flavors. "Holy smokes, that is delicious."

"I'm so glad you like it. Did you do anything exciting yesterday?" Ivy handed it to me, and I took a small bite. It was very good. I knew it would be. Growing up, my family frequented the pasty shop near our house, and I was excited to find it was still up and running. I handed the pasty back to Ivy, who took it with glee.

"We went to Buckingham Palace."

"Really? I was there yesterday too. Albeit briefly. It's too bad I didn't *bump into* you."

Ivy snorts a laugh as she chews. Wow, I like her.

"So, I have an idea," I start. For the first time since she sat down, I'm unsure. Not only that she might think it's a terrible idea, but that it might actually be. I could be setting us up for heartache in a week or so. But I feel like it's my only chance.

"What is it?" she asks at my hesitation, before taking another bite.

"Let's pretend we're in a relationship. Knowing it isn't real.

Knowing at the end of your trip, we will go our separate ways. I just ... I want to spend time with you. I like you; the reasons we wouldn't work are valid, but I don't see why we can't enjoy some time now while we have it."

"You ... so ... what? I thought you might suggest we be friends while I'm here, but you want us to pretend we are dating?"

"Yes. We have meals together. I can show you around a bit. Maybe you can help me with my riddles, whenever I get another one of those."

"*Friends* do those sorts of things," Ivy said.

"They do," I concede. "But I think we have too much chemistry to stop at friends. We would be fighting it the entire time. Why not embrace it?"

She turned to look out at the grassy park. "But ... what about other things couples do? Like—"

I slide my arm around her shoulders and pull her to me. "Like this?"

"Yes."

I turn and nuzzle my cheek against hers and whisper, "And this?"

"Mmm hmm," she breathes.

I lean back and catch Ivy's eye as I twine my fingers with hers. "This?"

She nods, looking back toward the park.

"Yes, I think a pretend relationship would have lots of these encounters. And similar," I say, and her eyes shoot back to me. I wonder if she is thinking about kissing, like I am. I run my thumb up and down her upper arm. "What do you think?"

She swallows. "I think it would be awfully hard to remember it was fake. I don't want to get attached and go home with a broken heart."

"We'd have to remind each other."

"You think that will work?"

"I think if it's not, we can reevaluate what we're doing. We can check in with each other."

She stares at me in thought.

"I'll buy you all the fish and chips you want."

This makes her grin. "You drive a hard bargain."

She looks down at her lap and the remnants of Cornish pasty sitting there. "You're going to spoil me, aren't you?"

"Oh, absolutely. My pretend girlfriend deserves everything."

"Hang on. Is this what you did with Grey Blankenship?"

"That was totally different. Fake just isn't real. Pretend is more."

"I don't know about that."

"Okay, maybe it's technically the same. But it isn't. I promise." I remove my hand from hers and trail the backs of my fingers down her cheek. "I did't mean it with Grey."

"I know you meant that to be reassuring, but that's what I

worry about. We can't mean it too much."

She's right, and I get it, but just sitting with her these past minutes has shown me that it would never be pretend for me. I'd come into this hopeful that she would change her mind at the end, but thinking I could move on without heartache if she didn't. I was wrong, but I'm going for it anyway. Just the chance she will change her mind is worth the risk.

"I'll remind you and we won't let it get too real."

She leans into my hand, which had turned to cup her cheek. Her voice is soft and threatens to give me chills. "I'll pretend with you, Alex."

Now here's hoping I can show her what it would be like to be loved by me and that she deems it worth it.

20

IVY

I THINK HE MAY have hypnotized me. He looked at me like he was either trying to stare into my soul or take control of my mind and force my mouth to form the word yes.He didn't though. There was no force. Only an earnest request delivered with such hope in his eyes that my only option was to agree.

"Can I take you to lunch?" Alex asks, a look of disbelief on his face, like he's still afraid I'll say no. Or he can't believe I agreed to his ridiculous idea.

It would be a lie to say I'm not worried. His display of affection almost left me once again ready to have twelve black-haired, half-English babies. I've got to put in some kind of protection, or I won't stand a chance.

"Hang on. I think there needs to be some kind of rules. For

our protection." He sits back a bit, loosening his grip on my shoulders, but not letting go of my hand.

"Ok. Name them."

"We can't be touching like this too often. I know actual dating would involve this sort of stuff often, but I think there is a fine line over into confusion. I think keeping touches to a minimum would help us stay on the right side of the line."

I don't miss the hint of disappointment on his face. "That makes sense. Okay."

"And no kissing."

"Hmm ... can we come back to that?"

I laugh. "No."

"What if we just say ... no kissing on the lips?"

"What, so you can kiss me on the neck? I don't think so."

"It would be good."

"I'm sure it would. Thus, the need to say no."

"I think I know a kiss that will be alright." He jumps to his feet and holds out his hand to me, a huge smile on his face. I place my hand in his and stand. He kisses the back of my hand. "How was that?"

"I think that's in the safe zone. In moderation," I add.

"Good. Any other rules?"

"No."

"Then how about lunch?"

"Yes, boyfriend. Take me to lunch."

A hole-in-the-wall sandwich shop was not where I expected Alex to take me for our first "date." And I'm pleasantly surprised. It reminds me of my restaurant with the exposed brick and similar seating. Similar seating to what *was* there, anyway.

I order a BLT after the woman behind the counter assures me the bacon will be crispy. I can promise you'll never find soggy bacon in my restaurant. Or in my mouth.

I watch as Alex approaches the counter. He had put on a ball cap, and never really looked up at her, keeping his eyes on the menu on the counter. She looked at him curiously, but recognition never lit her eyes. I'm glad I don't have to go to places and hide. I wouldn't necessarily call myself social, but I would miss the opportunities to smile or be kind to someone.

I walk toward the tables as he's paying. "Hey, Brad!" I call, just in case. "Do you want to sit by the window?"

He turns and looks at me with laughter in his eyes. "Sure, Betty, whatever you want."

He gets to the table and hands me a wrapped cookie he secretly bought me.

"I didn't even see these up there," I say, already unwrapping it and taking a bite.

"Dessert first?"

"I just wanted to taste it. You wanna try?" I hand the cookie to him and watch as he takes a bite and has an underwhelmed reaction. It wasn't great. "So what is it that you do, Brad?"

He laughs, setting the cookie down between us. "I'm a librarian during the day and at night I'm a bouncer at a nightclub."

"Wow. What a range you've got there. Do you see a lot of your library patrons at the nightclub?"

"There's surprisingly little overlap." Alex laughs. "What about you, Betty?"

"I'm a stay-at-home mom to forty cats." I grin. "And, unrelated, how much do you earn from your two jobs?"

He bursts out laughing, and I worry as heads turn in our direction.

"Keep it down. People are looking."

He shakes his head, smiling, and, man, he has a nice smile.

"So, you said you had somewhere special to take me. What is it about this place?"

"My grandfather brought me here every Saturday for lunch." He shrugs. "Well, most Saturdays, anyway. He always bought me bubble gum at the counter. But he made me wait until after I'd eaten." He eyes the cookie, and I laugh, wishing they'd had bubblegum at the counter instead.

"That reminds me of my grandfather. He didn't live nearby, but every time he came to town, he took Val and me to eat at one of like three or four places, and each of them sold York Peppermint Patties at the checkout. He always got us each one. I smile every time I see one of those at a check-out."

He smiled and nodded. "Same with bubblegum. It makes me wonder about what restaurant candy I'll buy for my grandkids one day."

Good gosh, we can't be talking about his black-haired grandkids. So I change the subject.

"You know, I've never been able to blow a bubble with bubble gum."

"I could teach you," he offers with a glint in his eyes.

"No way. We will not be doing that." I laugh.

"Let me know if you change your mind."

I shake my head, and the movement reminds me of how crazy my hair is today. I run my hands down it, trying to nonchalantly achieve some sort of calm.

"I love your hair. It's your showstopper, I think. It draws people in, then when you look closely at everything else, nothing disappoints."

Pretend boyfriend. Pretend boyfriend. Pretend boyfriend.

21

ALEXANDER

"A‍LEX, THIS IS INSANE."

"I want to have a fancy evening with you, and you didn't bring a fancy dress. So it's not insane for me to buy you one."

"I feel like I'm in *Pretty Woman*. It's gonna be clear I don't belong here."

"I never saw that movie, but you're definitely a pretty woman. So …"

She playfully backhands me in the abs. Conveniently, I had just exhaled, and they were flexed. I watch her notice that fact and turn away. I chuckle.

"Hello. And welcome. How may I help you today?" The woman spends ninety percent of her greeting time looking at me. It annoys me because we are in this women's boutique to shop for Ivy. But she doesn't react to my presence, so points to her that she has the good sense not to act like a big fan. Or maybe she isn't a fan, and that's fine too.

"I need a dinner dress," Ivy says. Clearly, she noticed the woman's attention was focused on me and wanted to get the woman back on track to what she should be doing, and who she should be paying attention to.

"Alright. Come with me. Sir, you can wait in the lounge outside the dressing room." I followed the direction of her lifted hand to an area filled with tufted chairs and proceeded to wait. My phone vibrates in my pocket just as I sit.

GRAY

> What are you doing in a women's cloth-ing store?

ALEXANDER

> How do you know where I am?

I look at my message settings with Grey and sure enough I've been sharing my location with her.

ALEXANDER

> Remind me to never let you use my phone again.

GRAY

> *crying laughing emoji* Don't worry, I'd never use it for nefarious reasons.

I *un*share my location.

GRAY

> Rude.

GRAY

> So really… What are you up to? Are you with Ivy? *big smile emoji*

ALEXANDER

> I am, actually.

GRAY

> SQUEAL! That's so exciting! I want the details!

I'm trying to formulate the words to tell Grey about Ivy and what it is we're doing when Ivy comes out of the dressing area. And she is stunning. Don't get me wrong, she has been absolutely beautiful in her more casual clothing, but there's something about how the dress hugs her curves that makes me stand. It's green, a shade darker than her eyes, and as I approach her eyes pop, but I notice concern.

"What's wrong?"

"It's so short. The woman assured me it was appropriate, but I have never worn anything this short."

"We don't need to get this one if it makes you uncomfortable, but I have to say … you have incredible legs, so if any of your discomfort is self-consciousness, there's no need for that. I promise."

I run the back of my hand down her bare arm because I can't not touch her right now, and smile as I see gooseflesh pop up in the wake of my touch.

"I'll keep it as an option." Her voice is a near whisper, and it makes me want to touch her again. To hold her and whisper to her about everything I find incredible about her. But I don't. Keeping my word to keep the touching to a minimum will be the most difficult part of all this.

"Good," I say before returning to my seat.

She comes out several minutes later in a red dress and I swear my heart stops for a moment. You'd think I would be immune to beautiful women, but there is something about her beauty that's real and pure, and that you don't find in Hollywood. At least I haven't seen it. And that it's the packaging of this incredible, funny, and smart woman. It's almost too much.

Once more, I'm on my feet.

"You like this one too?" she asks, and I realize I haven't spoken.

I clear my throat. "I like it very much. Do you?"

"Yes. I like this one and I think I like the green one too. I made friends with the length when I got back in front of the mirror. Which should I get?"

"We'll get both, and if you only wear one while you're here, that's okay." I slide my hands into my pockets to put something between them and the beauty standing three feet from me.

"That's silly; I don't need both."

"I'm going to buy you things. It might not be real," I whisper, stepping closer. "But we're pretending like it is and if you were mine, you'd have both dresses, and anything you wanted."

"You can't buy me, Alex."

"I know that. But I can't help but want to give you things."

She gives me a soft smile. "Well, thank you. I love them. And this one is so soft."

I look for anywhere I can touch it without stepping over a line she might have.

"It looks soft." Maybe I can touch the back.

"You can touch it." She takes my hand and brings it to her waist, and I groan internally. I never should have touched her in this dress. The fabric glides like water, and the warmth of her skin underneath sends my nerves into a frenzy.

"It's better than soft." I've never been more excited to make a purchase.

She smiles, unaware of my inner turmoil. "It is." She turns, heading back to the dressing room. "I'll be back in a minute." She throws a smile over her shoulder, and man, if it doesn't make my heart pick up even more speed.

I'm in trouble if I can't convince her to make this real.

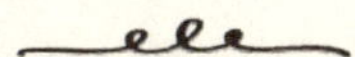

I dropped Ivy off at her hotel to see her family and get ready, and by the time I got home I decided to have dinner here. I asked Mrs. Brown to cook, and she was as thrilled about it as I knew she would be. I went to mum's garden and cut some flowers. I put them in a vase, and while I'm no florist, I think it looks nice.

I've showered and changed, and now I'm knocking on her hotel door.

It opens and I'm expecting Ivy, but instead, I look down and find Peter.

"Anizey's almost ready," he says before turning and going back to the sofa where Juniper is watching a cartoon I don't recognize.

"Hey, Alexander," Val says as she walks into the room.

"Hello—" I begin, but Ivy walks into the room and, despite having seen her in the dress earlier in the day, the breath is stolen from my lungs. She's worn the green dress and done something with her eye make-up that makes them stand out even more. She's nothing short of stunning.

"She looks good, doesn't she?" Val says as I continue to stare.

Ivy shakes her head and grabs her bag. "Ready to go?"

"Yes." I'll go anywhere with you. "You look more than good. You're—" Ivy looks a little uncomfortable and I remember our audience. At least I hope it's because of the audience, because she is going to have to get used to compliments from me.

I extend my hand to her, and she takes it.

"I'll see you guys later," Ivy says, and leads me out the door. And, like I assume our lives would always be if we were truly together, I follow her because my heart leaves me no other choice.

22

IVY

"THIS IS YOUR HOUSE," I say stupidly as I stand by Alex's car. Instead of parking in the garage, he's parked by the front door, so I stand there looking at his house instead of the fancy restaurant I'd expected.

"Are you disappointed? I'd intended to take you out when I asked, but the more I thought about it, the more I was excited to have you here where we wouldn't have to deal with people."

"So I didn't need this dress after all."

"No. You needed the dress." He gives me an appreciative glance, and I feel warmth flood my cheeks. "And I tried to make dinner nice for an at-home meal. I don't think you'll be disappointed."

My gaze lingers on Alex. "I'm betting there's not much

that's associated with you that could be labeled 'disappoint
ing.'"

He grins, then leads me inside where we're met by Mr.
Brown. "Good evening, sir. Miss. Your table is this way."

He turns and walks toward the dining room, and we follow
behind him. "Mrs. Brown must have put him up to this," he
leans in and whispers to me. I turn and come face to face with
his heavy five-o'clock shadow. I lose my mind and consider
reaching up to touch Alex when Mr. Brown startles me.

"Can I get your chair for you, Miss?"

"No." Alex's answer was a bit too forceful, making both
Mr. Brown and me stare at him comically. "Thank you, Mr.
Brown. I'll take care of it." He corrects.

"As you wish, sir."

As you wish. What does he think this is, *Downton Abbey*? I
laugh at myself internally.

Alex pulls out my chair and gestures with a flourish. "My
lady."

Once again, I'm laughing on the inside. I suppose he also has
been getting *Downton Abbey* vibes.

"It's really beautiful in here," I say, looking around.
"Strangely, I feel like I'm in a fancy restaurant." I grin, reaching
out to touch the petals of the blue hydrangea blossom. "This
is a beautiful arrangement."

"Thank you. They're from my mum's garden."

"You made this?" I'm shocked and delighted.

"I cut the flowers and put them in the vase, but I think Mrs. Brown messed with them after I left. They look better."

"Looks like you chose the prettiest blooms. Could I see the garden after dinner?"

"I would love to show you her garden. And you should take these with you when you go," he offers.

"I'd love to." I surprise myself with my agreement to take them. I'm honestly not very good at accepting things. Alex had to work pretty hard for me to let him buy me not one, but two beautiful, and I'm certain very expensive, dresses. I suppose, after that, the flowers are nothing. Though they're equally beautiful.

Mrs. Brown comes in with our salads. "Hello, Ivy. Lovely to see you again." She sets our bowls in front of us, along with what appears to be a flight of dressing options.

"Nice to see you too, Mrs. Brown. This looks amazing. You've made a beautiful salad."

"Thank you, dear. It would be an awful shame to have to eat an ugly salad," Mrs. Brown says before stepping back toward the kitchen.

"It would be an awful shame to have to eat an ugly salad. I can see that being on one of those decorative quote signs on a kitchen wall."

"What's a decorative quote sign? I mean ... I guess it's exactly what it says it is. I've never seen one."

"You've never been in a house with a decorative quote sign?"

"No."

I look around the room. "Well, you did grow up here, and I imagine you have a fancy man-house in California."

That makes him laugh. "Yes, you could probably characterize my house back there as a fancy man-house. So can you give me some examples of what one of those signs might say?"

"Hmm … well, Val has one in her kitchen that says, 'In This Kitchen, We Dance.'"

"*Do* they dance?"

"It's not something I've witnessed, but I get a feeling Val tones down her wild child when I'm around." I take a bite of my salad and chew while smiling.

"Huh. Why would she do that?"

I blow out a little breath. "I practically raised her. I'm not that much older than her, but maturity-wise, there were always years between us. I think she wants to prove she's a responsible adult now."

"Do responsible adults not dance in the kitchen?" he asks between bites.

"I like to dance and sing in the kitchen."

"You're a singer?"

"I enjoy singing, but only to myself."

"You'll sing for me one day, won't you?" The hope in his

eyes simultaneously brings me joy and reminds me of reality.

"I'm not sure we'll get to *singing* in our numbered days, pretend boyfriend." I say this to remind myself, but also to remind Alex, because the looks he's been giving me since he saw me at the hotel tell me this isn't as pretend for him as it is for me. Or at least as pretend as I need it to be.

23

Alexander

We make it to the garden right as twilight settles across the sky. It looks like the dream of every romance movie set designer.

Work your magic, golden hour.

"This is incredible." Ivy pauses where she stands on the pebble path that winds around the garden. "Your mom did all this?"

"She did. It was her passion. It's honestly the reason I don't think I could ever sell this house." I take her hand, and she allows it.

"Did you inherit her passion for gardening?"

"I don't have her green thumb, if that's what you're asking. But I deeply appreciate the beauty of it and understand the joy she found in creating something beautiful."

"I'm guessing creating is something you enjoy too, given your line of work." Ivy reaches out and touches the ivy growing on the stone wall farthest from the house, and I'm suddenly very glad her name is Ivy. It suits her. She could have been named for any one of the stunning flowers in the garden. Her name would have been well suited to her beauty, but personality-wise, she is more like ivy. She's not trying to catch every eye. She's content to let people walk past her, but when she sees someone she likes, she'll reach out and touch them. And I most certainly want Ivy to want to reach out and touch me. I need to figure out a way to encourage that growth.

"I do enjoy creating. Initially, I went to Hollywood to be more behind the scenes. I want to write or direct. But people saw me and wanted me in front of the camera. And I enjoy that too. I'm still a part of the creation, but ... I don't know. Maybe one day I'll make the transition."

"You'd want to entirely switch?"

"I don't know, maybe. I enjoy acting, but a drop in notoriety would be welcome."

She nods as if she's thinking but doesn't speak; she only continues around the garden. We come to a stop by the door to the house and she turns to give the garden another look.

"Thank you for showing me your mother's special place." She squeezes my hand that still holds hers. "I feel honored to have seen it."

I step closer and take my time tucking a bit of her hair behind her ear before leaning in and placing a slow kiss on her cheek. I linger a moment, basking in her nearness, before straightening to catch her eye.

"This felt like a must-kiss moment, even for a pretend couple."

"Mmm hmm. I agree."

She looks a little starry-eyed. A look that tells me she may let me kiss her for real. But the stakes are too high to jump in too soon, and I'm not going to risk doing something she doesn't want—or does, but may regret later. So I open the door for her to lead us back inside.

We're sitting on the sofa in the living room watching a movie, the candy and popcorn I bought strewn out on the table in front of us. Ivy sat down on the far end of the sofa from me and that's okay. Why? Because that tells me she's feeling things.

"Do you know any of the people in this movie?" she whispers, looking at me across the divide.

"Yes. I know both main characters. I went to a Halloween party at Chip's last year."

"One of my servers at Bowl had a Halloween party last year,

and I went."

"So you went to a coworker's party like I went to a coworker's party. That's what you're saying?"

"Yep." Ivy turned her eyes back to the screen.

"Except I've never worked with Chip."

She shrugs, keeping her eyes on the film. "You work in the same office; you just have yet to overlap on a project."

"Fair enough."

We're minutes from the ending credits when my phone buzzes in my pocket. I pull it out to find a text from Mr. Crawley. I hold on to it until the movie ends.

"That was good," Ivy says, scooting to the edge of her seat, like she's getting up.

"It was. I just got a new riddle from my aunt's solicitor."

She looks at her phone. "At ten-thirty at night?"

"I think she must have been very specific with the timing of the messages." I shrug and hold my phone out for her.

"Chaucer tells us a great tale. So old you feel you need chain-mail. The city has walls and inside you will find. A large and beautiful, building divine." She looked up at me when she finished reading. "The last two lines don't really rhyme."

I laugh. "She's been hit or miss with her rhyming for this whole thing."

She looks down at the screen, thinking, and I don't mention that I already figured it out. Aunt Agnes gave it away with the first line, but apparently Ivy hasn't read Chaucer's famous work. Ivy seems like the type to like to solve riddles, so I'll let her have some fun.

"Some sort of preserved medieval city, or town? And Chaucer, I've heard of him, but I don't know what he wrote. Wait. Wasn't he that guy in *A Knight's Tale*? The guy who likes to be naked. Or maybe that's just how I remember him."

"He did make an impression. I'm not sure his character in the movie is any help to us here, though."

"Oh! I wonder where the movie was filmed. That could give us a hint." She pulls out her phone, and I wonder if she's onto something. I have no idea where the movie was filmed, but I'm glad to follow along as she plays detective.

"It definitely could. It's been a very long time since I saw that movie, so I have no idea."

"The Czech Republic." She looked up from the phone, disappointed. "I'm guessing your aunt didn't want you to go to the Czech Republic."

"No. I'd say she didn't. Why don't you look up Chaucer, the actual person?"

She works on the phone for only a moment before excited eyes fly to mine. "Canterbury! She wants you to go to Canterbury!"

I grin.

"You knew," she rightfully accuses.

"Yes, Chaucer gave it away for me, but I thought you would have fun figuring it out."

"*Did I* figure it out? You told me to look up Chaucer."

"I had to contribute something to your search!" I grin and catch the pillow she flings at me. "That was fun. Maybe you can help me with some more of these before you go."

"I'd like that. But tell me if you already know the answer."

"I make no promises."

"So where is Canterbury? Is it far?"

"It's about an hour and a half from here."

"Oh." She looked a little crestfallen, like she'd wanted to join me, but felt like that was too far.

"You could come with me tomorrow."

"I don't know, I've already been away from my family all day today. And we have plans in the morning."

"We could leave when you're finished. Why don't you check with them and see what they think?"

"You think they'll tell me to go with you, don't you?"

I shrug. "I hope they will."

"They love me. They will want me to stay with them."

"Or do they love you so much that they want the best for you and know the best is going with me?"

Ivy shakes her head and smiles. "I guess we'll see."

24

IVY

"YOU HAVE GOT TO go with him to Canterbury. This is a once-in-a-lifetime opportunity," Val says.

"This trip with my family is a once-in-a-lifetime opportunity," I insist.

Val continues, ignoring me, "Or, really, it wouldn't have to be once in a lifetime if you would let yourself love him. He could bring you here any time you wanted."

"Val!"

"Just go. And pack a bag. What if the next place his aunt sends you is out there and you need to stay the night?"

"Val."

"Oooo, pack the red dress. You never know when you might need something fancy."

"Oh my gosh."

"And don't forget toothpaste," she calls as I'm walking out of her and Micah's room.

Do I want to go with Alex? Yes. I really do, and that's why I needed my sister to tell me no. To tell me to be responsible and stay with my family. Although, I have no idea why I expected she would. Driving out into England with a handsome near-stranger sounds exactly like something she would actively promote.

It was late when I got back to the hotel last night, so I didn't have a chance to mention what Alex proposed until this morning, after breakfast, while we were getting ready to go to the London Zoo, where we planned to spend the day. I don't know why I told Alex we had morning plans. We had day plans. It was almost like I wanted to leave myself an opening, but not simply say yes.

I love zoos, but I'm excited at the prospect of seeing more of England. And, of seeing more of Alex. I've got to tamp that down a bit.

IVY

> Hey. You were right. Val is practically forcing me to go with you.

He answers almost instantly.

ALEXANDER

> Glad to hear you're going against your will. It only hurts a little…

I roll my eyes, but it also makes me smile.

IVY

> I have to make sure you stay humble.

ALEXANDER

> You've been humbling me from the beginning.

ALEXANDER

> I like it.

I wonder if I'm the only person to ever humble him.

IVY

> Could we leave at 2?

ALEXANDER

> Sure. I'll pick you up.

ALEXANDER

You might want to pack a bag, just in case. I'm assuming we'll be back tonight, but if she has planned a place nearby, it would be nice to be able to take care of it. If you're okay with it.

IVY

Wasn't it a couple of days between the last two riddles?

ALEXANDER

It was, but as much as my aunt was a loon, she was practical. But who knows, I'm assuming we will be back tonight.

IVY

Okay. I'll grab some things.

ALEXANDER

Maybe the red dress?

IVY

You and Val should join forces.

ALEXANDER

Thanks for the tip.

IVY

I'm so thankful you don't have her number.

ALEXANDER

Who says I don't?

"Val! Does Alex have your number?" I call across the hotel room.

"No," she calls from the living area.

IVY

See you at 2.

ALEXANDER

big smile emoji

The London Zoo is beautiful and thoughtfully laid out, and I think I recognize some spots from seeing them in movies. I'm so excited to be here, and I'm trying to see as much as I can before I have to leave.

But there is a gorilla nursing a baby by the observation window, and we can't seem to move on from them. It's truly the coolest thing. Juniper gasps when the mother slings the baby into the crook of her arm, and they run off. Baby gorillas are not fragile.

We go next to see the Galapagos tortoises and I'm so stoked to see them. Only we get there and there isn't a way to touch them. They are behind glass and nets.

"What in the world? I want to touch them," I gasp. "What if it's bad to touch them and the zoo where I touched them before was doing the wrong thing? I could have unknowingly passed some sort of disease to them. They are so old."

"Some of these are younger than we are," Micah says, looking up at a sign.

"What? Are you serious?" I look and, sure enough, two of them were born almost ten years after me. I thought Galapagos tortoises were all like a hundred years old. Which, now that I'm thinking about it, doesn't make any sense. New ones have to be born, and believe it or not, they aren't born already a hundred years old.

"This says they can live to be well over a hundred," Val says, pointing to an informational sign. "So if you come back when you are a hundred and ten, you can celebrate the youngest one's birthday."

I laugh. "Yes, I'm sure my hundred-and-ten-year-old self will be up for going to London to visit a zoo." I lean my elbows on the fence, trying to figure out which one is which. "I wonder if the zoo does birthday parties for big milestones like that. Seems like great marketing."

When no one responds, I stand to find that my family has moved on. I don't leave right away because I think I have identified the youngest tortoise, and he is ever so slowly walking my way. He turns, though, and pulls his front end on top of one of the others, who doesn't even seem to notice.

"You guys are weird," I call. "I'll see you in eighty years."

25

ALEXANDER

I THOUGHT ALL MORNING about ways to make the most of this little trip. Ways to make it really count in my quest to sway her to make this real. But here we sit in silence. It's like something crawled under my skin the moment I picked her up and swallowed up all my good ideas.

"The traffic's heavier than I remember, but it's been a while since I've driven out to Canterbury." Traffic. Traffic is the best I've got. We've got over an hour left in the car.

She only hums agreement, and I glance over at her for what must be the hundredth time in the last half hour. She is so cute over there snuggled in with all her "travel accoutrements" as she called them. She has a blanket, a small pillow, a huge water bottle, and a bag filled with snacks. So many that I think she must have been afraid I'd let her starve to death on our short trip.

I hear her digging around through said bag, then she speaks. "Would you like a Mars bar or a Crunchie?"

Honestly, I shouldn't have either, given that for my next role I need to look like a professional rugby player, and I'm already pushing it on the age, but I'm not going to decline. "You don't have a preference?"

"I've never had either. I just chose two candies. Your candy here is weird."

I laugh and let that slide. "I think you should try the Crunchie. Our Mars Bar is the same as your Milky Way, so you can have that anytime."

"Alright." Ivy smiles over at me, opening then passing me the Mars Bar. "Enjoy road trip snack number one!"

"What else is there?"

"You'll just have to wait and see." She bites into her Crunchie and groans as she finishes her bite. "That is incredible. Can I take candy home in my luggage?"

"I would assume so."

"Yeah. I did bring a whole big bag of pistachios over here with me. It should work both ways. I'll just have to give away some of my clothes to make space. And actually eat the pistachios."

"We could ship a box home to you. Oh! You could sell them

in your restaurant, like a little ode to your trip."

"It would cost a fortune to ship as many as I'd want. But I can easily stick some in my luggage and ration them."

"I'm shipping you some."

"Alex ..."

"I'm doing it."

She sighs. "Fine."

⟋⟋⟋

"You're telling me you weren't actually in a desert for that scene? You shot the entire thing in a studio?" The candy, or maybe more specifically the sugar, got us talking, and we've been going strong for the past half hour.

"That is, indeed, what I'm telling you."

"It looked so real."

"I know. They did a really nice job with it. It just wasn't worth the effort of taking all the people and all the things to an actual desert. Not for two short scenes."

"That makes sense. I'm gonna have to watch it again and see if I can tell." Ivy pointed out some rather large cows grazing in a field to our right. "Are there any other secrets like that that would surprise me?"

"Hmm ... in *Activate* the—"

"I haven't seen that one."

"Really? It's one of my most popular, I think."

"I'm not a fangirl, remember?"

This makes me laugh. "Oh, I remember. We've talked enough about me anyway. Tell me about your restaurant. What will be the same? What are you changing?"

"Okay, I'll tell you all about it, but first ... road-trip snack two." She pulls her bag up from the floorboard. "Chips! Or *crisps*, rather," she said rather with an English accent that made me chuckle.

"I appreciate your effort at accuracy."

"I do what I can." She laughs. "Which would you like? Ready salted or cheese and onion?"

"I'll take whichever is least intriguing to you."

"Ready salted." Like with the candy bar, she thoughtfully opens the bag for me. She's a good co-pilot. She opens her bag and tastes one of her cheese and onion crisps. "Reminds me a bit of sour cream and onion chips. I like it."

"I'm glad. These are just like plain salted chips in the US," I say before popping one in my mouth.

"I made the right choice then." She pops another chip in her mouth and finishes it before she speaks again. "The restaurant. So, it's a historic building on Main Street, so it's got exposed bricks on the walls. And the ceiling. Man, it was my absolute favorite. It's these huge white embossed tiles. They made the place look impressive. They were able to be cleaned and saved, thankfully."

"The people who owned the restaurant years before me had modernized things and it looked okay. I didn't hate it. but I think I want to embrace some of the classic look it might have had when it was built. I think I'm going for an understated classic design. I'm hoping the ceiling, and the food will be the stars."

"I love that you're embracing what was. Growing up here, I was surrounded by history, obviously, and since being back I've realized how I miss it. I'm not sure if it's seeing things through your eyes a bit, or maybe my aunt's diabolical plan is working, but I've realized how infrequently I see anything actually historical anymore."

"The US is fairly young."

"It is, but there is still history around, and I love that you're trying to preserve and honor your piece of it."

I see her smiling at me in my periphery and it makes my heart pick up the pace. If only I could make her smile like that all the time.

26

IVY

"You're under arrest," Alex says, then holds my wrists behind my back. I'm embarrassed to say how much I didn't hate it.

"What is my supposed crime?" I laugh.

"Having hair more beautiful than is allowed by law."

This made me throw back my head and laugh, running my skull into his collarbone.

"Agh." He releases my hands. "I knew it was bad, but surely I didn't deserve that." He laughs and steps around to my side. "This used to be a jail."

We are standing in front of a super old structure that has towers and went over the road, and it's where we are planning to eat an early dinner.

"No joke?"

"No joke." He holds out his hand, and I take it. "Ready to eat?"

"Yes. My *crisps* have worn off!"

We step inside and find a mix of old intricate brickwork and modern designs. It's truly one of the coolest restaurants I've been to, and it makes me want to find an old jail to turn into a restaurant—although it probably wouldn't have the same effect in North Carolina. I'm pretty sure our old jails don't have stone towers.

Alex orders the truffle mushroom ravioli, and since he has no idea it will be my third time, I order the fish and chips.

When our food arrives at the table, I smile at the crispy fish waiting for me. Alex laughs.

"Would you like to try mine?" He asks, holding out a ravioli speared on his fork.

I'm not a huge fan of mushrooms, but I may like them inside pasta. "Sure." He seems to want to make a moment of this, so I lean forward, maintaining eye contact, as I slide my mouth around the ravioli. And then I inhale weirdly, which could have to do with the truly gigantic ravioli I have in my mouth. What was he thinking? He could have cut it. I go into a coughing fit, the ravioli ending up in my hand as everyone within ten feet of us watches.

Well, it was like a scene from a movie, just probably not the one he'd intended.

"Oh my gosh, I'm so sorry. Are you okay?" His face looked a little more devastated than the situation warranted. Did he think I would hate him now that he tried to choke me?

I cleared my throat. "I'm alright."

"That went all to pot, didn't it?"

I laugh, because what else am I supposed to do? I look around and find that my near choking has drawn attention, and despite Alex's less than stellar disguise–his glasses and a fancy hat of some sort—there is more than one phone pointed in our direction.

To be honest, it makes me a little mad.

"Play along," I whisper before taking my napkin from my lap and standing. I walk several feet from the table before seeming to remember something, I turn back and call, perhaps a little more loudly than necessary, "William." He looks up at me, just as I'd hoped. "Will you order some water for me while I'm gone?"

"Sure thing, babe," he says, in an American accent, not missing a beat. He's a talented actor, after all.

I stand in the bathroom, just long enough to seem reasonable. As I wait, my mind takes me back to my feelings about him being photographed while living his life. I suppose he's used to it, but he obviously doesn't love it, and that fact made me so mad on his behalf. Part of me thinks I care a little too much for my liking, but caring is, or should be, a natural human reaction. I would care if I didn't know him, right?

Wrong. I would assume he chose the life he lives, and if he doesn't like it, he gets compensated well enough to deal with it. Am I harsh?

I make my way back to the table where a tall glass of water waits by my fish and chips. "Thanks, Will," I say before I sit down.

He smiles with a slight shake of the head. "I hope you enjoy it, Margo."

The water tastes like water, but what I do enjoy is the fish and chips. I make it my new goal to find the best fish and chips in all of England. When I tell Alex that, he laughs.

"You'll be trying fish and chips for quite a long time. I couldn't even begin to guess how many restaurants here serve the dish."

"Let's see," I pull my phone from my pocket. "What percentage of restaurants here, would you guess, serve fish and chips?"

"I mean, I have absolutely no idea, but I would say at least ninety percent of pubs and traditional English restaurants do."

"Okay. Google says there are approximately thirty-nine thousand of those."

Alex only nods, like sure let's go with it, and absolutely this is something we should pursue.

I use my phone calculator to multiply the total number of restaurants by the percentage Alex guessed. "That's just over thirty-five thousand fish and chips to try."

"That will take some time," Alex deadpans.

I put my phone down. "I quit. This is a journey to Mordor I don't think my body could withstand."

"It was a journey, Margo, to watch your dream be born and die in a matter of minutes. Hopefully your next one turns out."

I grin. "Thanks, Willy." I pop a fry, excuse me, chip into my mouth, and vow to myself to try to replicate this dish in my restaurant. Although, I'd have to try to make it with a Bowl-able spin. Maybe small pieces of fish on a bed of fries?

"Do you think your aunt wanted a photo of you in a specific place here?"

"I'm guessing not, but we could take multiple photos and see what works. Also, I don't know if you've noticed, but it seems your little fake-out scheme worked. I haven't seen any-one sneaking photos since."

"Ha. Look at me being a good actress."

He grinned. "Yes, you really nailed it, Margo."

I pulled my phone from my pocket. "While we were in the car, I made a list of places to see while we're here."

"Okay. Where would you like to start?" Alex asks.

"How about the Canterbury Cathedral?"

"Let's do it."

I never knew I was an architecture nerd. The Canterbury Cathedral is stunning. Even approaching the entrance, the façade is covered in inlaid statues of people who were important to the cathedral. Archbishops, kings, and queens. Even the iron gate in the center is impressive.

We walk into the main area, which I would call the sanctuary but I don't know what it's officially called, and it is breathtaking. The ceilings must be over seventy-five feet tall, and the care taken to craft all the details is mind-boggling. Even Alex looks impressed.

"Have you not been here before?"

"I have. I was a child, but still, I'm not sure the awe ever wears off a place as incredible as this."

Thankfully, it isn't crowded, and no one seems to notice the uber-popular movie star in their midst. We go about our business, taking it all in. We take a selfie with the high ceiling in the background, which Alex promptly sends to his aunt's solicitor. He doesn't respond.

I'm staring around one more time before we leave when I notice Alex on his phone.

"Did the guy respond?"

"Not yet. I'm booking us a float down the River Stour."

"Oooo! That was on my list."

"I know." He grins. "The only ones left today are at sunset. Is that okay? It would begin at half eight. We could head straight back afterwards."

"Sure. Book it!"

He grins at me before looking back at his phone.

"What should we do until then?"

He looks up briefly. "Find all the fish and chips nearby?" He grins mischievously before looking back down.

"We could," I concede, like it is truly an option. "Or we could walk around and see what we find."

"All booked." He slides his phone back into his pocket. "Sure, Margo. Let's go see Canterbury." He extends his arm to me, and I thread mine through it. As we walk, it dawns on me that the scenery isn't the only thing that makes me feel like I'm in a fairytale.

27

Alexander

We wind up and down charming cobblestone streets, taking in the medieval architecture and the creamy-colored homes with dark wood accents. All the while, a look of awe never leaves Ivy's face. She is as enamored with this place as I am with her. And her reaction to our surroundings looks so unlike the faces I see in Hollywood. That's not to say there aren't good people there; it's only that so many are jaded and so self-important that there isn't a lot of magic for them outside of themselves.

Ivy is finding the magic, and her happiness is spreading to me in ways I didn't realize I was missing. I take a photo of her as she's touching a stone wall.

"Can you imagine what these walls have seen?" she asks,

leaving her hand on the stone and turning to look at me.

"I can't." And I wouldn't have even thought to wonder.

She sighs and we continue down the street. "I'm really glad I came today. I wish Val and I had planned for more of our trip to be outside of London."

"Where else do you plan to go?" I ask, trying to conceal my hope to join them. It had been rather convenient that her hotel was twenty minutes from my home. But if they leave and I'm not invited? It will be much harder for me to do what I'm wanting to do.

"In three days," she pulled out her phone, checking the date. "Days are weird on a long vacation. But yeah, in three days we're taking a train to Edinburgh to tour around the lowlands of Scotland for a couple of days, before flying out from there.

"Hoping to see a kilted man, are you?" I push my glasses up the bridge of my nose.

"I'm not seeing any here." She eyes my blue canvas shorts. "So yeah. That's top priority for Scotland."

"I could get a kilt," I offer. I'm not serious, but I'd do it if she wanted.

"You do have the legs for it," she says, eyeing said appendages once again.

"Thank you." I take the opportunity to study her long legs for a moment. Her overall complexion is fair, but I can tell her legs have seen the sun lately, giving them a healthy glow.

They're strong and beautiful. "You have the legs for a kilt, too."

This makes her snort a laugh. I love it when she does that.

"Why, thank you." Her eyes are absolutely sparkling, and good grief if I don't want to spend all my time complimenting her. To lay the world at her feet. Joke with her. Laugh with her. Make her look at me the way she's looking at me now.

"Have I mentioned how much I love your hair?" I ask, reaching up and coiling some around my finger.

"You have. A few times." She gives a small smile, her eyes crinkling at the corners, and I decide then that those crinkles might be my second favorite feature of hers.

"Hmm ... this probably won't be the last time." I let her hair slip off my finger and watch the curl reform.

She smiles and shakes her head, but she takes my hand. *She* takes *my* hand. It's the first time she's done it, and I count it as a major win.

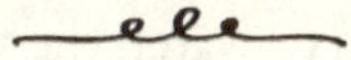

"Please. Just some small earrings. Or a bracelet if you'd rather."

"No," she whispers to keep from drawing attention. We wandered into Whitefriars, a crowded shopping area near where I had parked the car, and I brought her to a stop in front of a jewelry store.

"Come on, it's part of pretending. If this were real, I'd get you any jewelry you wanted."

"But when this is over, I would still have it, and I don't think I'd want it. And I already have the dresses."

"Oh. I understand. It would make you miss me." I nod as if this were an undeniable fact. And maybe it is, and this is simply another way she's protecting her future self. As much as I hate it and wish to shower her with gifts, I get it.

She just shakes her head and smiles up at me. "There's a man over there with blown glass. He's got a screen showing him making them. So cool. Let's go watch." She's clearly trying to distract me, and I let her.

We arrive just in time to see the recorded version of the man in front of us bringing the long tube with molten glass on the other end to his lips. He blows and spins and works the glass. I wish I could see it in person.

I pick up one of the finished pieces, a blue, white, and clear vase. "I'm going to get this for a friend back home."

I pay as Ivy continues to watch the video demonstration.

"So who is this friend who will love that vase?" she asks as we walk away.

"I hope she'll love it. I've made friends with a couple who own a restaurant that I love. I mentioned them when we were talking about your restaurant the other day. Mrs. Parker is almost always wearing this shade of blue when I see her. I'm guessing it's her favorite. And Mr. Parker is always buying her flowers, so I thought she could put it to good use."

"That was awfully thoughtful of you."

I shrug. "They're the best. Honestly, they're the closest thing I have to family now."

She gives me a sweet smile. "So do you just go around befriending restaurateurs?"

That makes me chuckle. "I'd not thought about it, but I suppose I do."

It looks like she's about to say something when we're interrupted.

"Alexander Henry! Oh my gosh! Can we take a picture with you?" Two girls, seeming to be in their early twenties, rush up and into my space. The girl who didn't speak shoulders Ivy back, then presses her phone into Ivy's hands without so much as a glance, much less a request of her.

"I would have been glad to take a photo with you; however, you running over here, pushing my friend, then shoving your phone into her hands, and disrespectfully interrupting our conversation has left me inclined not to." I take the phone from Ivy and pass it back to its owner. "I'm a person, and you're not entitled to my time just because you've seen my movies. And I certainly won't reward you treating my friends like they're invisible. Goodbye."

I turn from the stunned girls. Ivy looks at me, eyes wide, as I place my arm on the small of her back and lead her from the shopping center. I fume silently, until she stops, looks at me and smiles. "I'm gonna buy you a snack," she says.

She'd spotted a falafel street vendor and now leads the way toward the delicious-smelling foods.

We order chicken shawarma and falafel, and once again, I'm delighted to watch her eat. No wonder she opened a restaurant. She clearly enjoys food and the experience of trying new things. Her eyes light up when she takes her first bite of the shaved chicken and sauce in pita bread.

I want to take her everywhere just to feed her all the best food the world has to offer.

"Enjoying that?" I ask as I take a seat beside her. We've found a spot nearby on top of a short wall, away from the crowd.

She's still chewing, but she smiles and gives me a look that says *you know good and well that I am.*

Ivy finishes her bite, and I notice a drop of sauce on the corner of her mouth. I take the napkin from underneath the tray of falafel in my hand and slowly bring it to the corner of her mouth, cleaning the spot.

"You know, you could have just told me," she teases.

"And miss a chance like that? Bloody unlikely."

She laughs and knocks her shoulder into my arm. "I like your Englishness."

This makes me grin, falafel all but forgotten. "Do you?"

"Mmm hmm." She's acting coy, and it makes me want to

toss the food and press her back to the grass behind us.

"Well, as it happens, I quite fancy you and all your Ivyness."

A little color touches her freckled cheeks, but she laughs softly. "Eat your food, pretend boyfriend."

With her words, I notice a trend. I think each time she starts to feel something more, or something that surprises her, she calls me "pretend boyfriend." And yes, we did say we would remind each other of that, but I imagined it more randomly—not as much as a tool to try to shut down feelings.

I obey and take a bite of the falafel. I'm sure it was fine, but I didn't really taste it.

"I thought it was really good how you spoke to those girls." She wipes her fingers on her napkin. "You weren't mean, but you were clear that their actions were not what they should have been."

"I normally just take the pictures and move on, but I couldn't stand how they treated you. Acting like you don't matter."

I can tell she doesn't know what to say. If I told her how *much* she is starting to matter to me, would she try to push me away? I'm betting she would. Her hand is resting beside her, on top of the wall. I place my hand on hers.

"Thank you for letting them know that I matter," she says.

"Well, what kind of gentleman would I be if I didn't?" I joke, in order to keep myself from telling her how very *much* she matters to me.

28

IVY

ALEX KEEPS LOOKING AT me like I hung the sun, moon, and stars, and I need it to stop. He is sucking me into his vortex, and I need some way to fight the current. I don't know if reminders are going to be enough.

We finish our snack in companionable silence, then start walking to our boat tour. As soon as we do, Alex's phone pings with our, I mean his, next riddle. He reads it, then hands his phone to me.

The alabaster sights
Might cause some a fright
But Henry II
Loved it, I reckon

"People here say reckon?" I ask, surprised to see a word I hear back home, mostly from older, heavily southern-accented people.

"They do. I believe it's a British English word."

"Huh. I love it. I *reckon* I'll try to use it more often."

"You should," Alex encourages.

"Do you have any ideas about this one?" I ask, reaching my hand toward a bush just off the path to touch a delicate pink blossom.

"Actually, I do. I'm pretty sure she's talking about the White Cliffs of Dover. I believe Henry II built a castle there, but we should double-check before we rush off."

"Is it near here? It's going to be late and dark when we finish our float."

"I think it's half an hour or so from here. Further away from London."

I nod, processing this. Of course, it would make sense for us to take care of this while we are relatively nearby, but we'd really need to stay the night. Do I want to do that? Would my family care? Something tells me Val would all but force me to stay.

"I'd need to call Val, but let's do it. I'd love to see more of England."

His face lights up like it's Christmas. "Really? Are you sure?"

"Yes, but let me call Val."

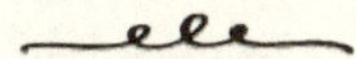

Val was, as I suspected, more than eager for me to stay. If I didn't know better, I would think I'd been ruining their vacation with my presence.

I give Alex the good news as he holds his hand out to help me into the gondola we will have to ourselves. He grins and keeps my hand as we follow the gondolier's instructions to our seats. I sit first, followed by Alex, who rocks the long, narrow boat with his size.

"Easy now, I don't want to end up in the water," I tease.

"I've seen what an excellent swimmer you are." He gives me a meaningful look, and it makes me think he is remembering the night at his house when he almost kissed me. Or I thought he almost kissed me. A kiss may never have been the plan, if there was one.

Just the thought of it has my heart picking up speed.

"This is beautiful, isn't it? I love when there's orange in the sky," I say, if only to distract myself. I close my eyes for a moment, enjoying the feel of the air moving around me as we begin to pick up speed.

"It really is."

Wisps of clouds fill the sky, streaked with corals and pinks.

I'm studying it carefully when I sense Alex's eyes on me and turn to him.

"I can see all the colors of your hair in this light. It's like it was made for the sunset."

I begin to make a flippant comment, but the look in his eyes is so earnest that I can't toss his compliment out of the window.

"Thank you," I whisper. Then drop my hand to trail in the water, then quickly remove it. It's very cold. "It's honestly really nice to get compliments on my hair. I've struggled with it my whole life. My mom certainly didn't teach me how to take care of curls. It's only been in the past year or so that I've found the right products and routine to make it look nice like this. Of course, depending on the weather it can still go wild on me at times."

"Tell me about your parents."

"I don't want to ruin this boat ride."

Alex only nods, looking mildly concerned.

"I'll tell you during our ride to Dover. Okay?"

"Only if you don't mind sharing. It's not my business; I just want to know you a bit better." He shrugs, and once again the earnestness in his eyes almost has me telling him my entire life story. But I keep my mouth closed for the time being because those words shouldn't be spoken in the presence of such a sunset.

"This is the Old Weavers House," our gondolier points out, pulling us out of our conversation. "As you can see, the sign says it was built in 1500, but there is evidence it could be even older than that."

"Wow," I whisper to myself as I look at the creamy building with dark wood accents. It reminds me of the buildings in *Shrek*.

I look toward Alex and find him studying the building and take a minute to study him. He said the light was enhancing my hair, but it's making him glow. I'm glad he's distracted. His black hair has slight blue undertones in this light, and his eyes are an even more striking blue. It's like they had been designed to match. Gosh, he's a beautiful man.

"Like something you see?" He smiles as he turns his eyes to me.

"There was a spider on your face," I answer in all seriousness.

"Why didn't you knock it off?" His eyebrows raise, playing along.

"I'm very strong. I could have hurt you. And let's face it, that's your money-maker. I wouldn't have wanted to leave you without a way to make your way in this world. I wouldn't be able to live with myself if you became destitute because I marred your face beyond recognition."

"Marred beyond recognition? Wow, you really are strong. But it sounds like a pretty good plan. I'll just move and live with you."

I snort a laugh, and I've never realized how often I do that until I got around this Englishman who grew up in a fancy family. I did it multiple times when we had dinner at his house and boy did it feel out of place.

"You'll be welcome with me should you ever become destitute."

"Thank you." Alex places a hand over his heart and nods solemnly.

We relax into silence as we continue to take in the scenery and ever-changing sunset. Alex's hand covers mine as we go through a low-clearance tunnel.

"This is really cool," he whispers, I assume to keep his voice from echoing off the stone.

"It really is," I reply, and he squeezes my hand. We come out the other side to find a duck swimming beside us. I look to Alex to make sure he sees it but find his eyes already on me. His breathing is accelerated, and as if he's moving in slow motion, he leans in as he raises his other hand to cup my cheek.

"Ivy. You're ... I've never felt ..." He rests his forehead on mine, and I feel his breath as it mingles with mine. I feel like I'm being sucked into a tornado. Totally helpless. That is until I feel the ghost of his lips on mine, and I jerk back.

"I'm so sorry," he says before I can sort through my feelings. Do I want to kiss him? Yes, of course I do. But is it going to be good for me, for him, long-term? No. It will just make things harder.

"Alex, you're not acting like this is pretend. It's like you forgot what we talked about." I glance up at the gondolier, thankful for the long boat and the fact that he has kept his back to us for most of the float.

"I didn't. Believe me, I didn't. I'm sorry. I got carried away with how right it felt to …" He sighs. "At the risk of sounding corny, I think I got caught up in the romance. I mean, you have to admit, this is perfect for a kiss. For a real couple, I suppose."

Did his accent just get stronger? It's like he's in a frenzy and any accent he may have lost while living in the States came back full force.

"You're not wrong. And I understand. I got caught up in it too. But, Alex, it would make it so much harder when we go our separate ways. You know it would."

"It's gonna be hard for me either way." His voice is nearly a whisper, but I hear it loud and clear.

I take his hand. "We don't have to keep doing this if it's too hard."

"No. I want to keep doing this. I want any time with you that I can get."

"Even if it's pretend?"

He runs his thumb along the back of my hand. "Yes."

"Okay, then." And then, I don't know what comes over me,

or if it's a good thing or not, but I lean over and kiss him slowly on the cheek.

29

ALEXANDER

I CAN STILL FEEL Ivy's lips on my cheek. I'm certain she didn't mean to, but that tiny kiss made things a thousand times harder for me. As much as I hate it, I'm glad she stopped me when I lost my better sense and tried to kiss her. I don't want to ruin this, and I think a kiss would have done just that.

Her lips on my cheek, though? I don't know when I'll be able to push it aside and stop wishing for more.

The clerk at the inn we are staying at, a tiny woman with short silver curls, hands us our keys with a grin. She'd recognized me and hadn't said anything, but it seemed she could no longer hold in her comments.

"I'll never forget the first film I saw you in. I said to my friend, 'He's quite tidy, isn't he?'" She giggles. Giggles. Like a schoolgirl. This is already in the top ten percent of my favorite fan interactions.

I grin. "I appreciate that. I hope you enjoyed the film."

"Ah. I've enjoyed all your films." She waves her hands, sort of shooing us away. "I've taken up too much of your time. You guys enjoy your stay."

"I'm sure we will. Thank you." I extend my hand to her. "And it was a pleasure to meet you."

"No, lad. The pleasure is all mine."

We're walking toward the stairs and our second-floor rooms, when Ivy leans in and whispers. "Did she just call you tidy?"

The next morning, I knock on Ivy's door. I texted her, but she hasn't responded. I don't want the breakfast in my hands to get cold.

She opens the door, and I am not prepared. Not in the least. Her eyes are half closed, an endearing grumpiness emanating from her pajamas. A black, pink-flamingo-covered tank top with matching hot pink short shorts. And as exciting as that entire situation is, it's, once again, her hair that draws the eye.

It's like she's been electrocuted. I cannot express how much I love the look. She must notice my particular attention to her hair because she deepens her scowl.

"Alex," she says in a tone that tells me I'm about to get scolded. That makes me smile in a way that I'm certain won't help. "It is eight-thirty. I'm still not adjusted to this time. Why on earth didn't you just wait for me to message you?"

"I didn't want your breakfast to get cold. I assumed since I have nearly adjusted, you would have too. I thought you'd be up by the time I got back with breakfast."

She stares at me, still blocking her doorway.

"I brought eggs and scones."She continues to stare.

"And lemon curd."

The staring continues.

"And clotted cream."

Her face doesn't change, but she takes a step back. "Come in."

***

"Still want to know about my parents?" she asks.

"I would, yes. Only anything you don't mind sharing." I peek at Ivy, all wrapped up in her blanket in my car, and I wish she could always be with me on adventures. I can't help but think she would be an amazing partner for anything and everything.

"Do I seem like someone who would let you force me into sharing something I didn't want to?" She grins over at me, and

I laugh.

"Definitely not."

She laughs. "Val and I never knew our father. To this day we don't know who he is. Our mother would never talk about him. As a child, I used to imagine he was an incredible man, who somehow didn't know we existed. You could believe that with one kid, but two?" She was shaking her head when I glanced in her direction. "Anyway, I would imagine he would come get Val and me. He would love us, and treat us well, and take me to snow tube on my birthday. That was a very specific dream. Birthdays were always a disappointment with mom."

"Did she not care about your birthdays?"

"She didn't really care about us in general."

"That's terribly sad." As strict and formal as my parents could be, I always knew they loved me and that I was their priority. I can't imagine growing up with a parent who didn't care.

"Yeah, well, it just meant that I was the parent of our family. Outwardly, it seemed like we had a great mom. She dressed us up and paraded us around. She loved to brag about her beautiful daughters. But it was all for show. She ignored us at home, and only talked to us as much as she deemed necessary when she took us places. Which wasn't often. Thankfully we lived in town, so Val and I would walk places just to get out. When I was old enough, I got a job so when I was sixteen, I could buy a car."

"What was your job?"

"I was a waitress. It's where I fell in love with the restaurant business. There's something extra special about it in a small town. I loved seeing the regulars. Remembering their *usuals*. I had one woman who wrote a Bible verse on every receipt she signed. I started bringing a notebook with me to work to copy them into since the receipts had to stay with the restaurant. Her name is Fran Randolph and she always got the soup of the day. It didn't matter what kind it was. And now she eats at my restaurant, and it's always a treasure to come across one of her receipts."

"Wow. That's really special." No wonder she doesn't want to leave home. I turn on my indicator before turning into the car park nearest the cliffs.

"It is. I'll be glad to see Fran when we get home."

"And your mom? Is she still around?"

"She is, but we don't see her. She seemed glad to see us go when the time came. Val's building her own family, and I ... well, I have my restaurant."

That makes me unexpectedly sad. I wonder why she hasn't married. Is she scared? She did say she has a hard time trusting. That makes a lot of sense now. Surely, she's met enough people to show her that there are plenty of people who are trustworthy. Or what if she doesn't feel like she deserves love? Maybe logically she knows that she does, but deep down her mum left scars.

I pull into one of the many open spots and decide against asking any of my burning questions. Not yet, anyway.

"You both came out of a bad situation and made something better with your lives. That's admirable."

She nods, seemingly lost in thought or memory—I'm not sure which. Either way, I feel the need to bring her back to the present.

"You ready to see the cliffs?"

Ivy has a death grip on my hand. We stand behind a fence at least five meters from the cliff's edge.

"Are you alright?" I ask.

"Yes."

For some reason, her weak answer doesn't have me convinced. I remembered her fear of heights on the Tower Bridge, but thought being here on solid ground, far from the cliff's edge would be different.

"What's that land over there? An island?" she asks as she stares across the English Channel, doing a nice job distracting herself.

"That's actually France."

She turns to me, surprised, and the grip she has on my hand slackens. I'm relieved that, at least for the moment, her anxiety has eased.

"Really?"

"Yes. You can't always see it, but it's a nice clear day, so there it is." It's a truly beautiful day, and the wind off the sea makes it nearly cool enough for a jacket.

"How far is it?"

"Hmm ... something like twenty miles? Perhaps more, I'm not certain. There's a sign over there." I point to a sign on the fence, and I take a step toward it. Ivy doesn't budge. I look at her and find her staring at something over my shoulder. I turn and find three teenagers over the fence, nearing the edge.

"Why are they doing that? What if one of them trips? Or even has a powerful sneeze? What if one of them is secretly mad—"

"Hey." I turn and take her other hand. "None of that is going to happen."

She has tears in her eyes. "You don't know that. It could definitely happen." Her eyes, which had been on mine, turn back to the teens. "We have to get them to come back."

Ivy looks as if she is trying to move, then instead looks up at me. "Will you go closer to them? Still behind the fence. Maybe take off your glasses and hat so they recognize you. They'll want to come away from the edge."

I want to say something to her about the wisdom of me taking off my glasses near a cliff, but I refrain. "Okay, sure. You want to wait here?"

She nods and as I'm stepping away, I let go of her hand, or at least I try to. I look back at our hands, then up at Ivy.

"I guess I'm coming," she says with an anxious and apologetic smile. I'm about to tell her something about not worrying or how sorry I am that I brought her here, knowing how bad the tower bridge was for her. Instead, she continues, "Let's get a move on. There are lives to save."

I lead Ivy slowly along the fence until we're as close to the teens as we can get without crossing. I take off my glasses and hat, then look at Ivy. "I'm afraid of calling out and startling them."

"See? Even you think anything could happen." She stands slightly behind me, both arms wrapped around my arm. I swear I feel her heart pounding against my tricep.

I'm contemplating how to get their attention when one of them looks in our direction. I wave, then wave him toward us. He takes a couple of steps toward us, then recognition lights his face, and he calls for his friends.

"Alexander Henry," the guy I waved at exclaims, in what I believe is a German accent, as he approaches. I notice Ivy relaxing her grip on my arm with each step they take closer.

"Hey, guys. I thought I'd say hi because my friend and I were a little worried about you all being so close to the edge." I turn to Ivy and she's looking up at me with the sweetest smile I've seen from her yet. I don't want to look away, but one of the teens speaks.

"Ah. We'd have been fine. But I'm glad you waved. Really cool to meet you."

"And," a girl speaks up, "you care enough to hope we don't die. That's awesome."

I'm about to open my mouth to tell them that while I do care, this was all Ivy, when Ivy speaks. "That's just who he is. He cares."

I look down at her with a teasing smile and lightly elbow her, which just sends her whole body backwards since she's still holding on to me. It shouldn't have been a problem, but apparently her feet get tangled and despite her hold on my arm, she starts to fall. I turn and get my other arm behind her in the nick of time.

"See? Anything can happen. I'm glad we weren't close to the edge," she calls to the group from where her cheek is pressed against my chest. They don't respond, and I can't tell you what their faces are doing because I'm too busy enjoying this moment with Ivy in my arms.

She steps out of my hold. "You guys want a picture with Alex?"

"We'd love that," the girl responds. "Would you mind taking

it?"

They climb over the fence and take several photos with me. Ivy seems to have forgotten where we are until the teens leave and the cliff's edge is once again in the forefront of her vision.

"There's a nature reserve where you can see the cliffs from below. Would you like to do that? I would have taken you there in the first place, but—"

"It's totally fine. We saved at least one life today."

I grin at her and her sparkling eyes. "We did indeed."

The only people we come across in Samphire Hoe nature reserve are an older couple wearing matching wool caps. They take a photo of Ivy and me in front of the cliffs. We'd seen them walking around holding hands and whispering in each other's ears. We thought, perhaps, it was because they were hard of hearing, but they heard us just fine. Ivy declared it *just romance*.

And hey, if it takes a lovely old couple to get Ivy thinking about romance, so be it.

"Did you send the photo to Mr. Crawley?" Ivy asks.

"I did. Right after they handed me back the phone."

"Good. I'm ready for another puzzle."

"Hopefully he sends it soon."

We walk along the beach, enjoying the blue waters and the view of the alabaster cliffs from below. And once again, *she* holds *my* hand.

30

IVY

ALEX IS MAKING THIS so hard. He is, by far, the sweetest and most thoughtful man I have ever come across. Walking with him by the English Channel, underneath the cliffs, felt like living through a movie montage of a couple falling in love. He held my hand, and he kept his hand on my lower back as we talked with the older couple who took our picture. I splashed him a bit, then ran from him when he threatened to splash me back. He chased me, catching me around the middle and spinning us on the sand.

It could not have been more romantic.

And now we are at Dover Castle, because instead of racing back to London and my family, I've decided to fully embrace this time I have to pretend-date the sexiest man alive. Literally, he was given that title two years ago.

I still worry about kissing him, but, good gosh, do I want to. I want to lose myself in his arms and forget my life back in North Carolina. But when I remember the restaurant and all I've worked for, I hesitate. To some, it may seem to pale in comparison to what could be with Alex, but to me it's everything.

"I've never been here before," Alex says as we stand within the castle grounds, looking up at the ruins of a two-thousand-year-old lighthouse. "So this is a first for both of us." He gently squeezes the hand he's holding, and I lay my head against his shoulder as I gaze up at the structure, which is about half the height it once was.

"Maybe we'll find some other firsts before this is all over," I say.

"It makes me sad to think about it being over. I know that's the plan, but I've lost control of things in my mind. If I ever had it to begin with."

"You said it would be fine," I remind Alex, turning to face him.

"I know what I said, but you make it hard to think about life after you're gone."

Everything inside me wants to say... You do, too. To tell him how I've been feeling, but I can't give him that hope. I can't give *myself* that hope either. So I lift up on my toes and kiss his cheek, hoping that will put off the sadness until I'm actually gone.

I pull my phone from my bag to check the time, and to avoid giving more meaning to the moment by catching Alex's gaze. I notice an email from my contractor. He's attached different design ideas, and the man has an eye for it. I had no idea! I pause to look at options for an embossed tile to cover the front of the counter. One of them reminds me of the ceiling tiles, only in miniature. It's got to be that one.

"What's going on over there?" Alex asks when I've been staring at my phone in disbelief for at least a full minute.

"My contractor sent me some design options. They must be further along than I expected. *And* he's a secret designer. I never would have thought. But he's got an eye for it!"

"Ah. So you like what he's doing?"

"Yeah. I really do." I show Alex the photos, and he swipes through them with a smile. I put my phone away, deciding to respond when we get to the car.

We're heading out of the castle, toward the parking lot when he gets a new riddle.

Remember, you might
A historical sight
A celebration was had
For your mum and your dad.

"The rhyming was on point this time," I say.

He chuckles. "She was showing her inner Elizabeth Barrett Browning."

"I was thinking Dr. Seuss, but whatever you think."

A laugh exploded from Alex as he opened the passenger door for me. "That is probably much more accurate. No offence to the good doctor."

He closes the door, then moves around the car and gets in.

"So I'm thinking I can't help with this one," I say as I buckle my seatbelt.

"No. But I know where she's talking about. We celebrated my parents' twenty-fifth anniversary in Rye."

"Where is Rye? How far is it?"

"It's west of here. I'm not sure how far."

He keys Rye into his maps app and finds that it's an hour from here. Once again, we are on the precipice of evening, and need to decide whether to go and stay the night somewhere, or head back to London.

"Let's do it." I'm committed to all this.

"Are you sure? You don't want to check with Val?"

"I'm sure, and I know exactly what she'll say."

I hear a text notification coming from my bag and pull out my phone. And what do you know? It's Val.

Val: Look at this.

It's a photo of the front cover of a tabloid. It looks like Val took it while standing in front of a magazine rack. The cover story features a photo of Alex and his ex-supposed girlfriend, Grey, walking hand in hand out of a restaurant. The headline reads, "Alexander Henry & Grey Blankenship back together? Our sources say, YES!"

I hold my phone out to Alex, and he takes a minute to look. "I'm not even gone a week and they're posting old photos and lies."

"To be fair, your whole relationship was a lie."

Alex laughs. "That's true. I just hope no one believes this. If photos of the two of us begin to circulate, people will think I'm a cheat."

I take my phone back from Alex. "You really do live in a different world. Do you think photos of us will get out?"

"Honestly? I'm a little surprised they haven't."

I nod, because the only thing I can think about is that this is exactly what I needed to remind myself that this is only pretend—and pretend is for the best.

It's dark and I'm so hungry by the time we make it to Rye. We'd stopped at a store, and each purchased new clothes and under-wear for tomorrow. I'd laughed and laughed as Alex held his five-pack of underwear, because these were, without a doubt, the cheapest clothes he had ever owned. "Welcome to real life," I said.

We walk into the historic inn where we'd reserved rooms for the night, and I can't help but feel like a dusty, saddle-sore traveler, who has stumbled into this place after a day of riding. Maybe I'm running from someone in the neighboring kingdom, and I don't speak the language of this one, but I know they will have a stew to warm my belly.

I have my back to Alex as he checks us in and orders room service. I'm mesmerized by the history in this small space. I look across the lobby to the restaurant, and if it weren't for the clothing and electricity, I'd think we had time-traveled. It's rustic and beautiful and part of me wishes we were eating down here, instead of in one of our rooms. But my head is starting to hurt, so I know we made the right call to stay away from the noise of the restaurant.

Our rooms are on opposite ends of a long hall upstairs. We go to relax in mine, and as we wait for the food, I decide to shower. He's already seen my flamingo pajamas, so what does it matter?

"They said thirty minutes, so you've got plenty of time," Alex says as he sits in the uncomfortable-looking chair by the window. "Enjoy."

I step into the bathroom and gasp. "There's a clawfoot tub!" I stick my head out the door and smile at Alex. "It's my dream to have a clawfoot tub!"

"A worthy dream, I suppose. I'm more of a shower guy, myself."

"This is just what I needed." I'll relax my headache away.

There's a sachet of lavender bath salts on the counter. Yes. This is *exactly* what I need.

I luxuriate in the bath for nearly half an hour. Only the promise of food could have gotten me out of the magic that is this tub. I'm standing on the rug drying when there's a soft knock at the door.

"I smell lavender out here," Alex says. Just the thought of him on the other side of the door has me smiling, despite the ache still present within my skull. "No rush, but the food's here."

"Oh, I'm rushing. I can't have you eating all the food before I get out there!"

I hear his chuckle through the door.

A moment later, dressed in my flamingo finest, I step out into the red-carpeted bedroom and find Alex standing by the table, which was covered in a truly obnoxious amount of food.

"What did you do? We'll never be able to eat all this."

"Darling, you underestimate how hungry I am. And you trusted me to place our order. I wanted to make sure I had some new-to-you things you would love."

I take a deep inhale. "Judging by the smell, I'm sure I will."

I finish towel-drying my hair and take the towel back to the bathroom.

"Judging by the bite of stew I just had, I'm sure you will."

I laugh to myself as I come back into the bedroom. They actually have stew for the weary traveler. I approach the table and find a few small pies, a tiny pot pie of some sort, the stew—which appears to have been served over mashed potatoes—a beautiful salad, and ... fish and chips!

In the end, we did not finish all the food, but we were close. As I'm eating, my head gets worse, not better, so when we finish, I tell Alex goodnight and send him on his way with the food tray. The smell is getting to me, and I'm regretting eating as much as I did.

I climb in the bed and over the course of the next hour of tossing and turning, my headache deteriorates into a migraine.

31

ALEXANDER

Something was off with Ivy tonight. I asked her if she was okay, and she said she had a little headache the food should fix, but it seemed like more than that. I hope she isn't regretting coming. I mean, she didn't act like she regretted anything. But she didn't seem at all like herself either. I think perhaps she was lost in her thoughts. I just hope they weren't sending her in the opposite direction from me.

I showered, and returned a few messages I received during the day, then went to bed. And now, I've been lying here for half an hour or so, but something within me will not settle. I turn on my side and try to focus on the good things, instead of worrying about what may be going on with Ivy. I remember the smell of the lavender coming underneath the bathroom door, and the feeling of domesticity the whole situation gave me. How real and right it felt, settling into a room with her. To wait as she filled the room with a floral scent as she got ready for bed.

I reach for my phone to check the time and find a message from Ivy sent fifteen minutes ago.

BEAUTIFUL IVY

Need you come help my please

I don't bother with a shirt; I just grab my key, sprint to the door, and fling it open. When I knock on hers, it's several agonizing moments before the door opens. Ivy must have been leaning on it a bit because she collapses into my arms.

"Alex." Her voice is so small and so weak; it crushes something within me.

"Shhh," I soothe, as I pull her up fully into my arms and walk her to the bed. "It's gonna be alright, darling. I'm here now and I'm gonna do everything I can to make you well again." I lay her down as gently as I can, then smooth her hair out of her face.

"Alex." Ivy reaches out her hand and grabs hold of my bare shoulder.

"I'm here, darling." She drops her arm and I place a soft kiss on her forehead. "Can you tell me what's wrong? What can I do?"

"Migraine." She takes a deep breath. "I need you to find medicine somewhere."

"Okay."

I don't have anything, but I call down to the front desk and see if they happen to have some or know where I can get some. The inn itself doesn't, but the woman at the desk has some in her purse and says she'll bring it right up.

I fill a cup with water and help Ivy sit just enough to be able to take the pill.

"I'm sorry. You should be sleeping right now," she says. In the darkness I can barely make out the tears rolling down her cheeks.

"No, darling, *this* is what I should be doing. I only wish you weren't going through this." I wipe the tears from her cheeks and hold her face in my hands. "It will be better soon." I kiss her cheek, then rest my forehead against hers, wishing there was some way I could take this from her. Transfer her pain directly from her head to mine.

There is a soft knock at the door, and I retrieve the medicine, thank the woman profusely, then go back to Ivy's side. I consult the bottle and realize I have no idea if she has any allergies. After confirming she doesn't, I help her take the medicine, but then I'm at a loss for what else to do.

I'm reaching for my phone to search for how best to help people with migraines when Ivy speaks.

"Can you rub my head and neck?"

"Of course." I look at how she is lying and consider where I should go.

Ivy starts moving toward the center of the bed. "Lie down."

She doesn't offer any explanation and simply waits for me to obey.

I do.

Once I'm settled, Ivy rolls toward me, resting her head on my chest. The feel of her cheek and her wild hair against my skin threatens to take me to places I don't need to go. She wraps her arm around my middle, and I think I want to be the one to help her through any and everything she ever has to go through. I want to be at her side to love and support her through everything she does. The good and the bad. Everything.

"Can you reach my neck and head like this?"

"Yes." My voice sounds broken, and I hope she doesn't notice. I bring my right hand to her neck and my left to her head. I'm not sure where on her head to massage, and I'm about to ask when I feel her relax against me. That's got to be a good sign.

She lets out a relieved breath, and I can't explain how it makes me feel to be able to help her like this.

I close my eyes and fight a shiver as her thumb starts softly brushing the skin at my side. I thread my fingers through her hair—like I've wanted to so many times—but with the goal of helping relieve any tension in her scalp. She hums and relaxes further, her thumb still branding me with the fire of her touch. I think I should get her name tattooed on that spot, so it will always be hers.

"Go to sleep, darling," I whisper, before placing a slow kiss on the top of her head. As if she needed my permission, she snuggles closer, it takes some time, but eventually I notice her breathing change as she drifts into dreams.

It's not long before I follow, hoping to meet her there.

I wake up cocooned with Ivy. She's facing me and I have her pulled against my chest. Right where she belongs. It feels like everything a morning should be. We'd gone to sleep on top of the sheets with the quilt pushed to the side, but apparently at some point in the night, we pulled it over us.

It's going to be hard to come back from this to anything pretend, so I hold onto her as long as I can. I stretch the night as far as it will reach, hoping that when those clear green eyes greet the morning, they will see me in a new light.

I'm on the verge of falling back into a contented sleep when I feel Ivy begin to move within my arms. I open my eyes, needing to watch her awaken.

"Would it make things more difficult if I said I never want to move from here?" Ivy closes her eyes again and runs her hand down my spine. It's all I can do to keep from kissing her.

"Probably. But if you'd like, I'll ask to buy the inn."

She laughs and rolls onto her back. "You would, wouldn't you?"

"For you? Absolutely." I prop my head up on my arm to look at her. "Migraine gone?"

"It is. Thank you. Actually, I normally wake up a little hungover after a night-time migraine, but I'm feeling surprisingly refreshed. I'm sorry I called you from your room, though." Ivy turned her head toward me, an apologetic smile on her lips.

"Trust me. I've never been less bothered by anything in my entire life."

"You slept okay?"

"Hmmm ... now that you mention it ..." I sigh dramatically. "I slept better than ever."

Ivy rolls her eyes and whacks me with one of the many extraneous pillows, then turns to her side, laughing, her back to me. I wonder how she'd feel if I slid closer and held her that way, but I don't get the chance to try. She sits up and stretches, her little flamingo tank top showing off bits of her perfect, creamy skin.

"It's so nice not to have a migraine," she says, arms over her head.

"I guess the food didn't fix your headache."

"No. It got worse and worse."

"I wish you'd told me before I left. I could have found medicine before it got too bad."

She stands and turns to look at me. Her morning hair, illuminated by the window behind her, is a sight I know would always make me smile.

"If I had, you wouldn't have ended up in here. Do you really wish that?"

I sit up, leaning against the headboard. "If it would have spared you any of your misery, yes, of course." Then I sigh. "And, also, it was a lot of work for me. I've never been a nurse before."

"You poor thing." She walks around the bed and sits on it by my knee.

I sigh again and shrug like I'm really put out but trying to act like it's no big deal. "I wouldn't say that you owe me, but if you felt you did, I would understand that."

Ivy suppresses a smile. "You know, I really do feel that way. And it just so happens that I have the perfect way to pay you back."

"Do you?" I'll take it. I don't care what it is.

"I seem to remember ..." She rises and approaches to sit

closer, then glides her hands excruciatingly slowly from my jaw to my neck and hair. "Your lips on me here." She slowly kisses my forehead. "And here." Her fingertips caress my neck as she kisses my cheek, then she stands, taking her hands from my neck and sitting them on my shoulders. "And here." Ivy kisses the top of my head.

I cannot help the earsplitting smile on my face as she straightens. I don't know what has got into her this morning but sign me up. "Are you sure that was it? I think my lips might have touched your lips."

"I'm sure they didn't."

"You were pretty out of it."

"I wasn't *that* out of it. Something tells me the feel of your lips on mine would be far too memorable."

And there was our problem. Or hers. I could live with only the memory. If I had to.

32

IVY

WHAT DID I JUST do? I close the door to my room behind Alex and press my back against it.

I'm not a seductress. I know Alex wants more with me, and I'm the one pushing against it. And then I go and do that. It wasn't fair to him. And it's screwing me up too.

"Ahh!" I push off the door and step to where my things sit on the chair by the window.

He held me and massaged me, kissed me, and called me darling for what felt like hours last night, and I woke up as content as I've ever felt. Lying there in his arms had felt so secure and wonderful. And, instead of panicking, I swung the entire other direction and told him I never wanted to leave, then seduced him.

Kind of seduced him. But still. I need to apologize. And make sure to remind him it's pretend. It's getting more and more difficult for even *me* to remember.

Why is it I can't give in?

Different worlds, and all that entails. Someone would compromise and be sad about it. I don't want that for myself, and I don't want it for him either.

There. I'm reminded. For now.

I ready myself for the day, gather my things, and head down to meet Alex at the restaurant.

As I come down the stairs, I see Alex waiting for me by the door to the restaurant. I cannot believe how beautiful he is. It's almost like he doesn't belong to this world. Even in his cheap store clothing, he looks like a million bucks.

Meanwhile, my clothes look like I closed my eyes and chose them at random. There wasn't a fitting room, so we each bought several items, hoping for the best. The blue-gray sundress I'm wearing is the best I ended up with, and it makes my boobs look weird.

Alex has his glasses off, cleaning them on his shirt, when I step up beside him and poke him in the ribs. He turns and smiles like I hadn't just given him the most childish hello to ever exist.

"Good morning, darling." He kisses my cheek. "Again."

My apology over breakfast went as well as you would suppose. Ultimately, it ended with him saying he would let me know if ever I did anything that went too far. Do I trust that? Definitely not.

The breakfast was simple, but delicious. And it included baked beans. I can't believe how long I've been in England and was just now having beans at breakfast. I have to say it was weird, but tasty nonetheless.

After we eat, we take our things to the car and proceed to walk around Rye to look for a great spot to take a photo. As it turns out, the place is *only* great spots for photos.

We take a selfie on Mermaid Street for the solicitor.

"This be a fair township," Alex says with a grin.

"What are you doing?" I laugh.

"This is a beautiful town, well village really. I don't know how to say town," he says. "I learned a bit of Early Modern English while filming—"

"*The Knight and the Darkness*," I say proudly.

"You honor me with thy knowledge."

I laugh. He really is funny. "Hast thou dispatched the pho-to?" I try.

"There weren't photos back then," he corrects, laughing. "But yes. Right after we took it."

I narrowly avoid tripping on a cobblestone.

"Would that we possessed a steed," Alex says, after observing my near fall. He takes my hand.

"So that we might ride it together?"

"Nay. So I might flee far from thee and thine advances."

I throw back my head and laugh. "How darest thou?"

A woman, old and bent, catches our eye. She's carrying an overfull grocery bag and can't get a door open. Alex releases my hand and hurries over to her.

"Excuse me, madam. May I help you?"

I approach to lend my femaleness in case she is worried about being approached by a male stranger, but she seems completely at ease. Whether unafraid, or simply unconcerned about the possibility of meeting her maker, I don't know. Of course, he had used exquisite manners, so she was probably charmed.

"My door is stuck. I've unlocked it, but it won't budge. It's the humidity."

She moves out of the way, and Alex opens her door with what looks like minimal effort. The doorway leads to a steep, narrow staircase, and I hope this isn't a place the woman has to come often.

"Thank you," she says, taking and squeezing Alex's hand.

"You're very welcome. Can I carry your bag up for you?"

I feel like he should carry her with her bag, but I refrain from offering that suggestion.

"Oh, no, thank you, dear. I do this every day. I go out for the morning shop and bring it up these very stairs. I've been doing it since William and I got married over sixty-five years ago."

"Wow. You've been married for quite some time," I say.

"When you're as happy as we are, it doesn't feel like a long time. But at the same time, I hardly remember life without him."

Alex smiles, then looks at me, and it wouldn't take a mind reader to know where his thoughts have gone.

Before either of us responds, she continues. "I've got bread to bake, so I must be off. But I thank you again, sir." A woman on a mission. She starts up the stairs, but before we get the door closed between us, she turns. "You two are a lovely couple. I hope you hang on to each other and have seventy happy years."

Alex thanks her, while I'm thinking about how we likely won't be here in seventy years. At least I hope not. I don't want to be one of those people on the internet celebrating a hundred-year birthday. Dentures falling out when I blow my candles.

The door firmly closed; Alex turns to me. "Well, we certainly can't disappoint her."

I shake my head as I step back to the cobblestone street.

Alex pulls his phone from his pocket. "Behold! He did send us a fresh riddle."

"I think we've done enough of that." I laugh. "What does it say?"

> India and China collide
> Where a king is no longer inside
> Alexander Benjamin Henry
> You stay away from the beach!

"What in the world?" I ask.

"There's a nude beach in Brighton. She wants us to go to the Royal Pavilion."

"But steer clear of the naked people on the beach."

"I shouldn't have told you. You're gonna want to go, aren't you?

"I might be confident, but I'm not that confident. But mostly, I prefer my eyes unburned."

"What?"

"I imagine some of the things there would make me want to burn my eyes," I say.

"Burn your eyes? Wow."

"There would be no other option."

Alex shrugs. "I'm pretty sure I'd only see one person on the beach."

"You don't think it would be busy?"

"I'm sure it would be."

Oh.

Alex looks at his phone. "It's an hour and twenty minutes from here. What do you think? I could take you back, if that's what you wanted."

"No. I called Val this morning and she told me I wasn't welcome back."

"Have I told you how much I like your sister?"

I shake my head. "Let's do it."

Green rolling hills slowly turn into neighborhoods and then to a cityscape as we drive into Brighton. It's a beach town not unlike ones I might find back home. Apart from, you know, a two-hundred-and-something-year-old palace, and such.

Alex's phone has been beeping at us for the last several miles. I want to ask him if I can just read the messages to him, but I don't want to overstep.

We park somewhere that's supposedly not terribly far from the Royal Pavilion and walk. It's lunchtime and I find a street vendor while Alex goes off to find a restroom. I'm standing in the Mr. Taco truck line when a man steps in line behind me.

"Hello, beautiful," he says, and I'm not certain who he is talking to, but there doesn't seem to be anyone else near enough. I ignore him.

"I'd love to buy your tacos," he says, stepping forward to stand by my side.

I'm not sure if this guy is friendly and interested in me, or a creep who likes to pick up women at food trucks. I'm leaning toward the latter. He's sort of giving off those vibes. Not that it matters; the answer's the same either way.

"No, thank you. I'm here with someone."

He looks over my shoulder, as if searching for my mysterious someone. "You can be here with me," he says as he runs a hand down my arm.

That hand was quickly knocked away before I could do it myself, and a large body forced itself between me and the stranger. Alex.

"You forget yourself, sir. Step away from my girlfriend."

I'm sure the guy recognizes Alex, but he doesn't say anything. He just walks away, probably to give another woman unwelcome attention.

Alex turns to me, and I watch his face transform from anger to concern. "Are you alright, darling?"

"I'm fine. He only touched me the once."

"Only? He shouldn't have touched you at all."

"Well, of course. I'm just saying, you saw everything bad that happened. I'm over it, truly." What I'm not over is Alex stepping in and getting rid of the guy. It was so hot. Was it necessary? Maybe not. What was that guy going to do in this busy place? I believe I could have sent him on his way. It might have taken some zingers and some glaring, but he would have left me alone. The way things turned out was better, though. So much better.

I smile as Alex slips an arm around my shoulders and kisses my temple. "Good." We step forward in line. "What kind of tacos are we getting?"

33

ALEXANDER

"This is, by far, the most interesting building I've ever been in. And I had no idea it existed. It doesn't feel like we're in England anymore." Ivy's eyes are huge as they dart around the Royal Pavilion.

"It doesn't," I agree.

"Do you know they do weddings here? I saw that on the website. I wonder how much that costs."

"So, you're thinking destination wedding? That's fine. I'll do whatever you prefer." Was I going too far? Sure. But while we're pretending, I might as well.

She rolls her eyes. "Alex."

"I'm pretending to be your boyfriend, and isn't that something a boyfriend would say?"

Ivy shakes her head, sending her curls bouncing.

My phone vibrates in my pocket. I'm sure it's my agent. He called three times when we were driving. I might as well take it while we're waiting for our tour to start. I hold up my phone. "I'll be right back."

I walk to an area free from people. "Hey, Isaac. What's going on?"

"I've got good news."

"Wait. It's just after four in the morning there. Why are you up, calling me?"

I hear papers rustling on the other end of the line. "I couldn't sleep. You know how I get when things are really happening."

"Yeah. I do." My agent never stops. I don't know how he lives the way he does.

"So anyway, I got a call last night from a casting director. He's working on a film based on what I've learned is the most popular fantasy novel in the world, and they want you for the lead. This would be your biggest role yet, and it's a series. And the money. We didn't talk specifics, but it would be mul-ti-multi-millions per movie. And there are five books."

He's wanting me to do five major movies? I glance over to where Ivy stands several feet away studying the design on the wall. If I'd been given this news a week ago, I would have been excited. I enjoy working and the process of creating. But now?

My priorities have had a sudden shift. Still, if Ivy is set on pushing me away after this, why shouldn't I take this?

"How long do I have to think about it?"

"What's there to think about? I've been looking into these novels for most of the night. You'd be perfect for this, trust me."

I do trust him. He's never let me down or led me astray, but things have changed.

"I do. But that's a big commitment. I want to think it through."

I hear Isaac sigh. "Alright, man. Take a month. They'll wait for you. But if you know sooner, please go ahead and let me know."

"I will. Thanks, Isaac."

We begin our tour, and I enjoy watching Ivy's expressions as we move from room to room. Her eyes are wide and her mouth often hangs open. We're standing in The Banqueting Room. Everyone's silent, apart from our guide who is telling us about King George IV's feasts, when I feel the need to sneeze. The thing is, I don't just sneeze. I do it in such a way that if I'm indoors, people worry the building might fall down. So far, no one has given me a second glance. There is so much to look at here that I've gone unnoticed. Ivy would give no credit to my hat and glasses.

My eyes water and nostrils burn as I try to stop the sneeze.

Unfortunately, my anonymity is about to go out the window. The sound reverberates off the walls—of what has to be the most echoey space in the building—and every head in the room turns to me. There is a chorus of "Bless Yous" and "Gesundheits", half of which fade out toward then end as, I'm assuming, they realize who has been lingering at the back of the group this whole time.

"Alexander Henry?" an older and, if I'm not mistaken, French man asks.

"Ah, yes. Hello everyone." I give a small wave to our group of fifteen or so. The tour leader looks at me like I have stolen his audience, and he isn't pleased. "So sorry. You were telling us about the chandelier. It is truly remarkable."

"Oh, yes. Please tell us more," Ivy adds, and thankfully that was all the encouragement our tour guide needed.

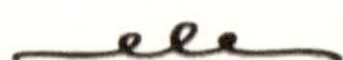

After our tour, we take photos outside the palace with many of the members of our tour group, including the, for some reason, all-important group photo. These people acted like we had become best friends during a week of summer camp and were saying goodbye. We have a woman take a photo of just us in front of the palace and I send it on to Mr. Crawley, who, of course, doesn't respond.

"What now? We could make it back to London by half five or so."

"I'd like to see more of this place."

"I'd love that, but ... are you sure?"

"Yeah. I want to go to the pier," Ivy says, looking at her phone where she has already searched for the attractions in Brighton.

"I'm sure you can't see the nude beach from there, if that's what you're hoping for."

Ivy burst out laughing, which fills my entire body with happiness. "That is too bad. I was very much hoping to see a large amount of sagging skin today."

It takes us less than ten minutes to walk to the pier, Ivy holding my hand the entire time. She bursts out laughing when we arrive.

"What?"

She points to a sign near the entrance: Fish and chips. Of course.

"Are you hungry?" I ask, but she is already pulling me in the direction of the food.

"No. But we have to try it. We'll share. It'll be an afternoon snack." She paused. "Tea! It will be our tea. Totally English."

He laughs. "Sure. Totally English."

We get our food and head onto the pier. The wooden deck is covered with games and rides. An arcade sits in the middle.

The whole place is rather wild, yet Ivy's first comment is …

"It's so funny to me that it's called a toilet here. I mean, I get it, you aren't going in there to rest or take a bath, but still. It seems so crass. Toilets are gross." We watch as a woman walks out of the toilet. "Does that woman look like she just stepped out of a toilet?"

I just laugh. "Come on. Let's find something more exciting than a *restroom* to look at."

"Does such a thing exist?" She laughs, and I desperately wish I could snatch the sound from the air and stick it in my pocket so I could pull it out and hear it anytime I wanted.

34

IVY

THE SEA BREEZE DANCING around my ill-fitting sundress makes me nearly forget my sundress is ill-fitting. This vacation is turning out better than I could have ever imagined. I got to spend time with my family, and I'll do that again soon, and I've spent time with Alex, who I'm certain I'd be falling in love with if I weren't so stubborn.

As much as he might draw me in. As much as I might want to give in, ultimately, I know what I'm keeping us from is for the best. For both of us. It's just unfortunate that I'm the only one keeping us on this side of the line. I think he had folded without realizing it before he even suggested we pretend.

I watch as a mother and her two young daughters play hand games as they wait to ride the carousel. The mom pokes one of the girls playfully in her belly, and the girl giggles and squeals. "Mummy, stop being silly."

The girls remind me so much of me and Val. I feel like I'm watching a video of what could have been. How would our lives have been different? How would they be different *now*? It's taken me a long time to get rid of the it's-not-fair mentality I carried around for years. The fact is, our childhood wasn't fair, but there's no reason for me to keep dragging that around.

Alex leans over and speaks softly. "Thinking about your mum?"

I take my eyes from the little family before us. "How did you know?"

"Because I was." He squeezes my hand.

"The oldest one even has curly hair," I say, unsure how to handle my emotions as I stand by a carousel, its cheery music an odd backdrop for emotions I usually keep in check.

"I wish I could travel back in time and take you both so you could be in my family."

I give a weak smile at the mention of time travel. "I'd be kinda like a sister in that scenario."

"It wouldn't be an easy sacrifice, but I'd do it." He wipes at a tear that has just escaped my eye. "You know, you've turned your life into something far beyond what you were set up to do. You're successful in doing something you love, you're kind and thoughtful. I imagine one day, if you have children, you'll be everything your mum wasn't. You're incredible for having overcome—"

"But I'm not sure that I have. I have so many issues, most of them centering around the fact that I can't trust people. And sometimes I think I work so hard because I want to rub my success in my mother's face. I want to say, 'Look what I did, no thanks to you.' That's not healthy."

"You could already do that if you really wanted to, and you haven't. You don't need to strive for anything you don't truly want."

"I know that. At least I think I do. It's just hard not to want to punish her in some way."

"Your mum has missed out on you and Val, and her grandchildren. I'm sure no matter what she does to fill it, her life is empty."

Alex puts an arm around my shoulders and leads me further down the pier. We're looking out at the water from the end of the pier, my head on Alex's shoulder because, why not? I feel his phone vibrate against my hip. He ignores it, but I can't.

"It might be another riddle."

He gives me a funny look.

"I felt it," I inform him.

"Ah. Alright, let's check." He lets go of my shoulders, and as much as I hate to admit it, my mood instantly drops. It's not that I was suddenly depressed, but there was a noticeable difference. Good grief.

"You were right." Alex holds out the phone so I can see.

> Once a farm
> Also a prison
> Now the gardens
> You cannot miss 'um

"That one's bad," I say.

Alex nods his head in agreement. "This is going to take some Googling," Alex says. "Unless you happen to know."

I give him a look that says, "Yeah, right."

We find a bench and search, until we decide the answer might be Sissinghurst Castle Gardens, which is an hour and a half from where we are.

My gaze is to the ocean. "We could go in the morning." I turn my eyes to Alex. "It would have to be my last stop."

"I could take you back tonight if that's better for you." He says the words like he means them. Like he wants to do what's best for me and my trip, but there's a sadness behind his eyes that I don't miss.

I put my hand on his knee. "Let's find something fun to do tonight."

We leave the pier and end up at The Lanes, which are narrow alleyways lined with shops, restaurants, and pubs. And, once again, we find ourselves standing outside a jewelry store.

Alex turns to me with a huge grin and pleading eyes.

"Alright. You can buy me something," I concede. I don't feel a lot of fight in me at the moment. He pulls me into a hug, and I'm sure he's reading too much into me allowing this. Still, I'll take it. It feels too good to be hugged. Especially by Alex. He's so big, I feel like I'm being totally surrounded.

He releases me and takes a small step back, then runs his hands over my wild hair. "Thank you."

"Shouldn't I be thanking you?"

"No." Alex takes my hand, and we walk into the store.

"No diamonds," I whisper, and Alex rolls his eyes.

"That's fine. I think you need an emerald to match your eyes."

The store is opulent. That's the only word I can think of to describe the level of luxury before my eyes. There is nothing *cheap, but good enough* here. Most of me hates to think about what he's fixing to spend, but I'd be lying if I said there wasn't a little part of me that felt like a kid in a candy store. I've always loved jewelry, but I've never had anything real. Only cheaper items, or ones that may look real to the undiscerning eye, but certainly aren't.

"Are you sure about this?" I'm again whispering to Alex, like we aren't allowed to talk at normal volumes in this store. And, honestly, calling it a store doesn't seem right. It's more like a museum. People whisper in museums, don't they?

"I'm absolutely sure."

Alex tells the finely dressed woman behind the counter—who pretends not to know who he is—that we want to see anything they have featuring emeralds, the lighter in color, the better.

"What if I want a dark emerald, or ... a ruby?" I tease.

"We can get whatever you want."

The woman brings out a selection of jewelry featuring emeralds, ranging from crystal green to grass green. I point to a pair of earrings: simple, thin gold chains that lead straight down to teardrop-shaped emeralds. I hold them up to my ear, looking in a mirror. They're perfect.

"They're beautiful, but would they be hidden?" He twists some of my hair around his fingers.

"I could wear my hair up," I suggest.

"I'd like to see your hair up." He looks at me like he's trying to imagine what I would look like with my hair contained on top of my head. "Are they what you want, or do you want to keep looking?"

I know myself; if I kept looking, I would get overwhelmed and never be able to choose. "I want these. They spoke to me instantly."

Alex smiles and kisses my temple. "Then they'll be yours."

He pays, and I purposefully stay away. I don't want to know the worth of what would at some point dangle from my ears. As we walk out, he takes my hand in his and lifts it to his lips for a soft kiss.

"Wear them tonight?"

I look down at the blue-gray sundress. "I'm not sure this is the right outfit for them. For multiple reasons."

"Did you bring the red dress?"

***

I had, in fact, listened to both Alex and Val, and packed the red dress. I pull it out of my bag at our hotel for the night and find it fairly wrinkled. Of course. I let it hang in the bathroom while I shower, then leave the water running as I smooth my hands down the dress, and to my relief, the wrinkles relax.

I pull my hair into a wild poof on top of my head, making sure to leave some tendrils around my face. I'm giving my cheeks a little color when my phone lights up.

VAL

So… kiss him yet?

I roll my eyes. Val is a hopeless romantic.

IVY

No. And you know why.

VAL

You could let yourself love him.

IVY

Love?

VAL

Sure. Maybe not today, but eventually, yes. Love.

IVY

You know why I can't.

VAL

You could be missing something that would outshine everything you think is good.

IVY

I can't talk now. He'll be here any minute, and I need to get dressed.

VAL

Just think about it. Or don't. ;)

IVY

Goodbye, Val.

I haven't told her how my emotions have been all over the place. How this very morning, I kissed him all over (apart from his lips, obviously) while he sat on the bed we'd shared for the night. Val doesn't need to know everything. I swipe mascara onto my lashes and pull on my dress only to find I can't reach the zipper. I twist, turn, bend and do all manner of things to close it, because this will not turn into one of those will-you-zip-me-up situations.

Nope. I couldn't handle it. And, thankfully, I won't have to, because I got it!

I'm back in the bathroom, putting in my new earrings when there's a knock on my door. I open it and find Alex standing there in a charcoal-gray suit, his white shirt unbuttoned just the right amount—and wow I might pass out.

He steps into the room, letting the door fall closed behind him as his eyes bounce around my form—taking in the dress, my hair, my face—before lingering on the line of my neck. He steps forward and runs his hands down the sides of my neck, and across my collarbones before he nuzzles just below my ear, the earring caught somewhere between us.

"You are so beautiful, darling," he whispers, then kisses me softly on the neck. He backs up a bit, leaving his hands on my mostly bare shoulders. "I hope that wasn't too much. I—"

"It wasn't," I breathe, once again riding the rollercoaster of emotions he brings out in me.

"Good." Alex uses his index finger to push his glasses up the bridge of his nose. "Ready?"

In this moment, I feel shockingly ready for anything.

For dinner, we end up back at The Lanes at a *very* elegant restaurant. Alex, or I suppose his assistant, has arranged for us to have a table in the corner, out of the way.

Alex cuts into his steak and spears a bite along with a green bean—as he has done with every bite he has taken since we finished our appetizer of truffle and parmesan chips.

"Why do you always eat a green bean with your steak?"

"There's something about the flavor of these green beans that I don't like. I found that I don't notice it when I eat them together."

"You could ask for another side."

"I don't want to make a fuss. Also, the only other vegetable they have today is creamed spinach. I'm not generally a fan of that."

"You're a little bit picky," I joke.

"I prefer to say I have discerning tastes," he said, putting on airs.

I nod. "That makes sense. You do seem to have a thing for me."

I expect him to laugh; instead, he leans closer, and I feel his hand on my knee beneath the table. "I'm afraid it's becoming more than a thing, darling."

I know I should stop him right there. I should remind him that we are pretending. That there is no future for us. Come tomorrow, I will be gone. But I don't. I can't. I don't know if I'm only trying to enjoy the last of our time together, or if he has broken through my fears and the impossibility of it all. But his hand has me all out of sorts. I want it to live there.

"I just realized you're left-handed!"

His eyebrows raise. This was obviously the last thing he expected to hear.

"I was just thinking that it would be hard for you to eat if you kept your hand there since you're having to use a knife. And then I realized that it's your right hand on my knee and that it would be even harder eating with your left hand. But then I realized, because as you know I was watching you eat, that you were doing it left-handed."

He gives me a crooked smile. "Are you feeling nervous? Is it my hand on your knee?"

"I'm not nervous." Yes, I am. I'm nervous about how I'm

feeling. Or maybe anxious is more accurate. I feel his thumb slide softly against my knee. "I'm worried about saying good-bye tomorrow," I admit. This pretending—if it's even pretending for either of us anymore—has been better than I expected, which, of course, will lead to some level of heartache.

He's considering me, as if he's gauging how to respond. I can tell he wants to tell me tomorrow doesn't have to be goodbye, but he doesn't. Instead, he says, "Let's not let tomorrow ruin today."

He knows I know how he feels. I guess he doesn't want to beat that into the ground. Or, maybe, he hopes there will be something about tonight that will speak his feelings directly into my soul, and I'll be able to see past the roadblocks we would face.

It would be too easy.

I nod and cup his face in my hand in response. He closes his eyes when I drag my thumb slowly across his cheek. I lean in and replace my thumb with my lips and hear his breath catch.

I cannot believe the power I have over this man. Here he is—literally the dream of seventy percent of the world's single women—and there's something about me he likes well enough that it changes his breathing. Me. Small town, regular woman.

"You smell really nice," I whisper as I lean back. "I haven't noticed this scent before."

"I bought it today while you were getting ready. I went out in search of some perfume for you but decided that I love how you always smell. And perfume is probably something you should choose yourself."

I shake my head at him. "And you had already bought me these gorgeous earrings."

He takes his hand from my knee, then reaches and lets one of the gems rest on his fingertips. He lets it drop, then trails his fingers down my neck. "You're ..." He clears his throat. "You've always been stunning to me, but there's something about your hair being up and the curve of your neck that drives me a bit wild."

That last part, in combination with his accent, threatens to make me fall out of my chair. He rests his hand against my neck.

"Do I need to take my hair down for you to be able to finish eating?" I tease, trying to bring some levity to a conversation that was getting a little too romantic for my saying-good-bye-tomorrow self.

He slowly removes his hand. "Oh, darling. That would leave me distracted by your lovely hair."

35

ALEXANDER

IVY AND I ARE sitting in a pub, and I'm wondering at the wisdom of my suggestion that we sing karaoke. I know I must look like myself, dressed as nicely as I am. My glasses do next to nothing to disguise me. I know this. But when Ivy agreed to my plan, I was too chuffed to change it.

She and I are looking at song options, and I'm having trouble focusing with Ivy's arm brushing mine each time she turns the page of the book of songs.

"I have an idea." Ivy turns to me, a cheeky look in her eyes.

"Alright. What is it? A duet?"

"Nope. I choose your song, and you choose mine."

"That's dangerous. Especially for me, based on the look on your face." I cock an eyebrow at her.

She grins. "You would get to pick my song too. It's an equal risk."

"Is it, though?" I smile and look at her doubtfully.

"It will be fun," she singsongs.

"You've got yourself a deal." I hold out my hand and she shakes it. She steps back from the book. "I know what I'm picking for you, but I want you to go after me so I'm gonna wait for you to sign me up."

I shake my head and act annoyed by her control of the situation. "That's fine."

Ten minutes later, I'm sitting alone in the audience at our little round table, and Ivy steps onto the stage. Someone whistles, and I'm glad I don't know who it was, and I won't take the time to look. My eyes are glued to the woman on stage. Her eyes light up with laughter when she sees her song on the screen.

I chose *Lady in Red* by Chris de Burgh, because she is the lady in red and I hope she'll dance with me later. After karaoke, this place changes to a dance club and there's nothing I want more right now than to hold her in my arms.

Ivy has a lovely voice. She's not getting nominated for a Grammy, but still, I never want to stop listening. I'm mesmerized by the way the light hits her, illuminating the colors of her hair, and highlighting the curves of her body. It's like she was made to be onstage.

She sways gently as she sings, and I'm hit with an image so unexpected that it takes me out of the moment for a second. It's Ivy, still swaying, but with a baby cradled in her arms. My baby. My heart squeezes and I take a deep breath. Children have always been this nebulous idea, something I imagined would happen someday when I found the right person, but this feeling—this knowing—it's so strong. I want Ivy and this mysterious baby, and I don't care what I have to sacrifice to have them.

Because, in the end, I know it won't feel like a sacrifice.

When I step onto the stage, there is a period of silence when the clapping dies down, and then people realize who I am. Then people scream and clap louder, every phone in the room points at me. I can't sing terribly well. I'm not a musician, but I can see the appeal. The energy is electric.

I give Ivy a look like, *look I've already done better than you,* and laugh. Then I look at the screen and find my song. *Wanna Be* by the Spice Girls. Wow, Ivy. Well done. I look back out at Ivy, and she has her head thrown back in laughter. She thinks she has got me good. But she's forgotten one thing. I'm a performer.

I don't need the screen; those lyrics were burned into my

brain in primary school when every girl I knew dreamed of being a Spice Girl.

I danced and hammed it up for the crowd. For Ivy. I look at her every chance I get, and each time her smile threatens to knock me off the stage. My song ends to riotous applause, and I'm afraid they won't let me back off the stage. Back to Ivy. But they do. They make a path, and smile and offer high-fives, as I walk toward the green eyes that I can't wait to drink in.

I take my seat and Ivy speaks, only I can't hear her over the still-roaring crowd. She tries again, resting her cheek against mine as she leans in and whispers, "That's my favorite thing from this entire trip."

I chuckle. "Even better than fish and chips?"

"That's not a fair comparison," she says, but doesn't elaborate. She laughs as she leans back in her chair.

The crowd continues to be excited as we witness a moving, if more than slightly off-key, rendition of *I Will Always Love you*—Whitney Houston's version. And then karaoke closes with a bloody brilliant cover of *Locked Out of Heaven*.

Staff and patrons, me included, move the tables and chairs to the perimeter of the room to make a dance floor; then the lights dim, and music fills the air.

"Dance with me, darling?" I ask, once again having to lean in for her to hear.

"I would be delighted," Ivy responds in her best English

accent. Life with her would be fun and exciting. I know that for sure.

Guiding her onto the dance floor, my hand rests on her lower back, feeling the warmth of her body through the silk of her dress. My entire being is focused on that point of contact. At first, the music is energetic and playful. There isn't a lot of contact between us, but our eyes are locked in on each other.

After a couple of songs, the music slows, and I wrap Ivy in my arms, and she steps into me like she knows she belongs right here. A cover of *I Can't Help Falling in Love With You* is playing, and I'm hoping Ivy is paying attention. I hope she's thinking about falling in love. I know I am.

I trail one hand from her lower back up her spine to the skin I meet halfway, and she shivers. She had wrapped her arms around my middle, but I take them and slide them up my chest and leave them over my shoulders. I rest my forehead against hers for a moment as we sway. Then I kiss her cheek and speak into her ear, "You are *everything* I will ever dream about. I know you know I don't want this to end, but I want you to know that I will never get over this feeling. It's like I've been stumbling around in the dark, and then I bumped into you."

Ivy brought her hands to my neck and gently guided my head back to look at her. She stared into my eyes like she was trying to see my past and my future. The gentle touch of her fingers moving into my hair and down onto my neck, over and over, helps keep me grounded while I wait for whatever it is she's gonna say or do. I can't help pulling her closer, and when I do I see her gaze flick down to my lips. My heart rate instantly doubles.

Ivy tilts her chin up to me, then slowly brings her lips a breath from mine. "I wanna try this," she breathes just loud enough for me to hear over the music. I'm not sure what *this* she means exactly, but whatever it is, I'm up for it. Ivy slides her fingers into my hair and brings her lips to mine.

My world turns upside down.

It's like breathing for the first time.

Like all my hopes and dreams—past, present, and future—have met in this moment to explode like fireworks around us.

There's no longer any pretense of dancing, no longer a crowd around us. We stand, each of our movements solely focused on the other. I slide one hand up to the warm skin of her upper back and bring the other around to cup her face. I feel her hum against my lips and my breathing turns ragged.

It's as if I've been waiting for this my entire life, not for the past week.

"Ivy," I whisper before taking her plump bottom lip in my teeth and sliding my hand from her cheek down to her lovely neck.

Time passes in a blur of sensation until a hand, not belonging to Ivy, lands on my arm.

"Excuse me," a nervous male voice begins, "I'm afraid I'm going to have to ask you to leave."

Ivy looks mortified as the pub and the people come back into focus.

"So sorry," I say to the man, then take Ivy's hand to get my coat and leave.

Laughter is absolutely bursting from Ivy as we step out into the night.

"What's so funny?" I chuckle.

"Alexander Henry gets asked to leave a pub despite being uber famous. It just tickles me." She grins up at me.

"Excuse you. You got kicked out too."

"Hmm. I did." She looks pleased with herself, and that's all it takes to give me an idea.

36

IVY

It's after midnight. I should be exhausted, but Alex has my veins coursing with adrenaline. It's quiet out. The echo of our shoes hitting the bricks is louder than normal with my senses on high alert.

Alex holds my hand, and all feels right in the world.

Suddenly, he pulls me into a darkened doorway, and what the shop is, I couldn't tell you. Only that it is closed. Before I know it, he has me pushed up against the door, and good gosh if this isn't the hottest thing that has ever happened to me, or maybe anyone in the world.

"I have to kiss you again." His hands bracket my shoulders as our breath mingles. "We got interrupted, so I think really, we need to continue our first kiss."

"Good," is all I say because my mind is absolutely blank. But it's the understatement of the year.

Suddenly his lips are back home. Soft and warm against mine. I realize my hands are dangling by my side, so I grab his suit coat and pull him even closer. He cradles my head in his hands—leaning it to the side—then trails kisses across my jaw and down my neck, pausing halfway and whispering, "You are a dream."

Alex once again takes my lips with his, and I groan. He grabs hold of one of my thighs, the heat of his hand like fire through the silk. I shiver when he slides his hand up to my waist. We could have been doing this for a week now? My mind refuses to remember any of the reasons we hadn't been.

The first kiss had been filled with passion, but this one crosses over into frenzy. My breathing turns shallow as he threads his fingers into my hair and makes a sound that, I guess, would be considered a growl. I've never been the inspiration for such a sound, and wow, is it empowering.

I push his chest the two steps to the wall behind him, and he smiles as his back hits the wall. Gosh, that smile.

"I'm at your mercy, m'lady."

"Yeah, you are." I drag my hands down from his chest, into his coat, and grab hold of his sides. Alex wraps his arms around me. I go up on my toes to kiss him again.

"Mmm ... you're warm." I pull him slightly away from the

wall so I can bring my arms all the way around him inside his coat.

Alex brings a hand up to tuck some loosened hair behind my ear. "Are you cold, darling?"

Not anymore.

⁓

Clearly, my adrenaline has worn off by the time we make it back to our hotel. I open my eyes and find Alex leaning into the SUV, his hand gently stroking my cheek.

"Wake up, darling. You'll sleep much better in your bed."

What a way to be dragged out of a deep sleep, I'll tell ya. I would pay good money for this man to be my alarm clock. Obnoxious beeping is a thing of the past!

I lean into his hand. "Alright. I'm awake." I take a deep breath, turn my body and let my feet fall to the ground without realizing the rest of my body is following. Alex is there. Of course he is. I'm still wearing his coat he'd wrapped about me as we walked to the car, and I feel tangled in a mess of his arms and his coat. Not all tangles are bad.

"I've got you," he says as he sets me back on my feet. "Are you okay to walk?"

I step away from the SUV and close the door. "Perfectly

steady. Nothing like a little tumble to wake you up."

"You're sure you don't need me to carry you inside?"

I pat him on the chest. "As fun as that would be, let's save that for another time."

"Something to look forward to," Alex says as he threads my arm through his and leads me into the small hotel.

We walk in silence to my room. He pulls my key from his pocket. He'd offered to carry my things, and I jumped on the opportunity. Plus, I didn't have a fancy enough purse with me and, call me crazy, but I didn't want to give him another reason to buy me something.

Alex unlocks the door and pushes it open, holding it for me to walk in. "Do you need anything?"

I shake my head, but then say, "Maybe just a goodnight kiss."

"Haven't had enough?" he teases.

You know the saying, *too much of a good thing*? I'm not sure that applies here.

"Not quite," I reply.

He stands against the open door and extends his hand. I take it and he pulls me to him, keeping my hand. He lifts his other to cup my face, then kisses me with such tenderness I feel like the most precious thing in the world to him.

"Goodnight, darling."

"Goodnight, sparky."

He lifts his eyebrows in surprise or question; I'm not sure.

Either way, I'm not sure I hit the mark with my impromptu nickname.

I yawn. "I'll try harder next time."

ALEX

Let me know when you're up.

IVY

I'm up.

I've been up for at least twenty minutes, luxuriating in the soft sheets and snuggly pillow—which I'm going to have to ask about before we leave. I need one.

I hear my door unlock and realize he'd forgotten to give me my key last night. There's a little knock at the door and his voice comes through the crack. "Can I come in?"

I try to smooth down my hair and make sure my pajamas aren't twisted weird, then I pull up the covers. He's already seen enough flamingos on this trip. "Yes. Come in."

Alex walks into the room in his cheap clothes, looking yet again like a million bucks. "Good morning, darling." He's carrying a bag and two warm beverages. I really hope one of them is coffee.

"I've noticed you enjoying coffee the past couple of mornings, so I took the liberty. I wasn't sure how you took it, so there's cream and sugar in the bag with our food." He sits the drinks on the nightstand beside me and opens the bag, handing me the cream and sugar.

"And what are we eating?"

"Fish and chips, of course; what else?"

I throw my head back in laughter, and when I right myself, I find Alex staring at me. "What?"

"You're just so beautiful."

"Alex, I'm a mess. I didn't take off my makeup last night. I probably have mascara streaked all over my face."

"I don't see any, but even if you did, you'd still be beautiful. Startlingly so."

"You can't compliment me like that before I've brushed my teeth."

"Trust me, I think I could power through anything at the moment." He takes my hand and raises it to his lips. "But I'll wait to kiss you until your hygiene is at whatever level you'd like it to be. Your comfort is my top priority."

I laugh. "Well, I must care for your comfort too, because I would certainly hate for you to have to *power through* anything." I grin. "So, really, what are we eating? I woke up hungry."

"I got us sarnies." He sticks his hand in the bag.

"Um. What?"

"It's a breakfast sandwich." Alex hands me my paper-wrapped sarnie. I open it and find a bread roll filled with bacon, egg, and avocado. "I got one without avocado too. I wasn't sure if you liked it. And, not to brag, but I asked for the bacon to be crispy, like you like it."

I sit my breakfast on the nightstand, throw off the covers, and rise to my knees. I take a couple of awkward knee steps and throw my arms around Alex's middle.

He made sure I'd like the bacon.

37

ALEXANDER

We couldn't have asked for a more beautiful day to visit Sissinghurst Castle Gardens. The sky is a bright blue, and the warm sun is casting the gardens in the most beautiful light.

"I bet they have weddings here," Ivy says as we walk into the rose garden.

"That's the second time you've talked about weddings on this trip. What is it about you and me and ... weddings?"

With my arm around her, she gives me a playful shove with her shoulder and chuckles. "I was just saying that because it's beautiful and looks like a great place for *someone* to get married."

"Mmm hmm ..."

She rolls her eyes. She may not have been thinking about a

wedding involving the two of us, but I'm happy to make that connection. I can't help but dream.

I wonder if she'd like a fancy destination wedding. I want to ask, but I have to stop myself. She just now seems to be coming around to the idea of trying to make something real happen with me. I don't want to scare her.

"Which color roses are your favorite?" I ask.

Ivy had been studying the red roses growing on the brick garden wall, but she stops at my question to let her eyes search for her favorite. "I think those deep pink ones might be my favorite. I've never been a big fan of roses but seeing them grow like this may change my mind."

"What are your favorite flowers?"

"I like peonies. I like how they look ruffled and there are so many colors of them. I wish I could have peonies or an arrangement that included peonies in it at home all the time."

"You don't think you'd get tired of them?"

"I doubt it. I mean, the novelty might eventually wear off, but it would take a long time for that to happen, I think."

Ivy leans down to smell one of the roses on the wall, and I take a photo. I look at it, and I can see it printed in black and white and hanging in my office. I'm not, however, seeing my rarely used office in Malibu. I'm seeing some unknown office in my future. Maybe in North Carolina.

My phone buzzes in my pocket, I retrieve it and find Grey

has responded to a selfie I'd sent her of Ivy and me.

GREY

> Look at her hair! She is so pretty! When do I get to meet her?? *big smile emoji*

A large crowd shows up in the garden, so I think it's best if we move along. I pocket my phone. "Would you like to walk to the lake?"

She looks up at me, her freckles standing out against her pale skin in the sunshine. "I'd love to."

We step out of the garden, then take a selfie of the two of us in front of the main building—which I instantly send to Mr. Crawley. I take Ivy's hand as we walk through the beautiful grounds.

"Something about this place makes me want to take a picnic," Ivy says as the lake comes into view.

"We'll take a lakeside picnic one day. Although, I'm not sure fish and chips will be as good packed up and taken all the way to a lake."

Ivy laughs softly. "You wanna know a secret?"

"Of course, I do." I've never wanted to know a secret more.

"I think I've finally had enough of fish and chips. I mean, I'll want them again someday, but I think I've overdone it."

This makes me burst out laughing, startling a bird out of a nearby tree.

"It's not *that* funny." She smiles up at me, and I put my arm around her.

"Does this mean that *I'm* your favorite British thing now?" We come to a stop by the lake, and Ivy doesn't answer right away. We stand quietly, watching the ripples on the water, until she turns and slides her hands along my neck and into my hair, then tugs me downwards.

"That depends."

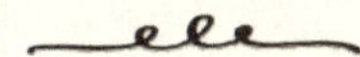

"I'm not going to want to say goodbye to you tonight," I say, setting down my tea. We're eating at the restaurant on-site. A young couple came to the table asking for a photo right after we sat down, but otherwise we've been left alone to enjoy our meal.

"Me neither, but I think it's time for me to be with my family. All our stuff is booked. There isn't space for another."

"I could take care of all that; you know I could."

"I ... yes, I know." Ivy sets down her fork.

"If it's that you want to spend the time with just your family, you can say that. I would understand. You've been off with me for much longer than expected." It would be discouraging, but understandable.

"It's not that. I mean, it's a bit about that. I want to make sure I'm considering their feelings."

"Of course. Why don't you spend the evening with them, and see how things are seeming? They may really just want to spend time with you, and I can certainly understand them wanting to have you to themselves."

She snorts a laugh, and I grin. I love it when she does that.

"I could see it going either way. Val is a hopeless romantic, you know."

"I do love that about her."

38

IVY

AFTER LUNCH, WE WANDER into the Sissinghurst Plant Shop
& Secondhand Bookshop near where we parked our car. I
obviously can't take home a plant, but I could, perhaps, find a
good book for the train ride tomorrow. Alex and I separate for
the first time today when I head toward the fiction section.

I'm debating between two books when I look up to find
Alex perusing the history section, a book about World War II
in his hand. I set my books down and walk over. "Do you like
reading about history?"

"Not usually, no. But I think being back here, surrounded
by history, has me thinking more about the past. And going
to all these places to get my grandfather's stuff has me wanting
to know about the world when he was my age." He held up

the book. "He actually served in World War II. He was barely eighteen."

"Wow. Really? Did he talk about it much?"

"No. And I was always curious about it. Well, once I became old enough to know about the war. I loved my grandfather, but he wasn't much of a talker. I think there was trauma there that wasn't dealt with."

"That often seems to be the case."

"It does. But he ... I wish he had said more. All I know is that he loved my grandmother before the war, they got married after, and it was a while before they had Aunt Agnes, and years later, my father."

"I imagine a book like this could help you feel closer to him. Like you could put yourself in his shoes a bit. Do you know anything about what he did in the war or where he went?"

"No. I mean, I'm sure I could find out some of it, but sadly I don't. I'd meant to ask my dad about it, but never got around to it. And now, obviously, I can't."

I reach a hand to his forearm, hoping to comfort him. "I'm so sorry." So sorry about his parents, so sorry about the missing information about his grandfather, and so sorry he's the only one left in his family. He needs people to love. Maybe it's me. Maybe it's the dozen black-haired, blue-eyed, accent-confused babies. Or it could be someone else. *That* doesn't feel terribly good to think about, but I can't quite leave behind all my earlier reservations, as much as I'd like to.

He gives me a sad smile, and it breaks my heart. I've never seen him less than neutral. Usually he is bright smiles, teasing and laughter. I feel the need to cheer him up. I lift onto my toes and kiss his cheek. "Come on. You're getting that book, but I want you to help me pick mine."

His smile is back. "I'm not sure I'm qualified to do that."

I pull him toward the fiction books. "Oh please, of course you are. You know a good story. I know you do."

He nods. "Alright. Do you have options, or are we working from scratch?"

"I narrowed it down to two." I hand him the first one, a fantasy romance involving a woman who's forced to marry a werewolf—before she knows he is a werewolf.

He reads the blurb on the back and gives me a look. "I mean, this doesn't speak to me in particular, but it could be good, I guess. Let me see the other."

"Was it the werewolf, or just fantasy in general that seems unappealing?"

"I don't like that she got tricked."

Ah. Good man. I hand him the second book, a romcom about a divorced, pregnant woman who falls for a military man from her childhood, who is suddenly back in her life.

He studies the back cover. "I think this is your winner. It seems like it could be fun with the pregnancy and all the craziness that goes along with that."

"All the craziness that goes along with that?" I laugh. Both of Val's pregnancies had craziness attached to them, so I don't think he's wrong. Just funny.

Alex laughs. "I don't know. I've not been close with any pregnant women. I mean, I've been around them every now and again, and I've heard stories, and seen movies and TV shows, so I get the idea. Although, if most of what I know about pregnancies comes from the screen, it's probably exaggerated."

I shrug. "I would imagine most of the pregnancy things are real; they may just not all happen to every woman."

"Makes sense." He stacks the second book with his, and we walk toward the counter. "Do you want to have kids?"

"I would love to have kids," I answer, and I don't miss the light in his eyes. Good grief, this man.

"Good to know."

We don't receive a new riddle from Mr. Crawley, but it doesn't matter. Either way, I need to get back to my family. I'd spoken to Val this morning, and even *she* was ready for me to get back.

She loves me after all.

I didn't mention the possibility of Alex tagging along for

the Scotland portion of our trip. More like the possibility of him hijacking and restructuring the rest of it. He probably already has his assistant looking into things. Honestly, I'm a bit surprised Val didn't suggest he come along. It makes me think she's ready for it to be just us. But then again, maybe it just hadn't occurred to her.

We drive back to London in comfortable silence; at least it begins comfortably. We stop for car snacks to share and pass them back and forth. I take Alex's phone and play music. But my thoughts ultimately turn back to logistics and the impossibility of it all. I know I should just talk it out with Alex, but I'm feeling irrationally embarrassed. I shouldn't, I know I shouldn't. But I do.

As we near London, I realize I'm not quite ready to leave him. Maybe a bit more time will be what I need to get rid of these thoughts. At least it would give me more time to work up to talking with him about how I'm feeling. "Could we go back to your house for a bit? They aren't expecting me until five."

"Can't get enough of me, can you?" he teases, but he's right. Now that I'm seriously entertaining the idea of trying to make something of us, I *can't* get enough of him. And I need to save up enough kisses to get me through until we're together again.

"It's your humility that draws me to you."

He laughs, turning on his blinker. "Thank goodness for my

exceptional, maybe even unmatched, humility."

I smile over at him, leaning my head back on the headrest. "Given how handsome you are, I almost couldn't blame you if you were the least humble person on the planet."

He laughed. "Right back at you, darling."

I reach for his hand, and he twines his fingers with mine. He rubs his thumb absently as we drive and the last twenty minutes pass in a euphoric blur. As we pull within sight of Alex's house, he straightens, drops my hand and puts it with the other on the wheel.

"What's wrong?"

"Paparazzi outside." There's an anger in his voice I haven't heard before.

I straighten in my seat and look around. I don't see a way to escape. Worry gathers in my throat, and I try to swallow it down. "Could we just drive past?"

"They know my car. I guarantee some of them have already seen us coming." He pauses. "They're already stepping into the street."

Before I know it, the car is surrounded. My heart is pounding in my ears.

They are beating on the window and hood, all clamoring for Alex's attention. Each beat on the car feels like a personal assault. Anxiety claws at me as they scream questions. Questions I can't understand until I hear my name. Not "who is this woman?" They know my full name. I feel like the walls are closing in.

I startle as a man beats on the window right by my head, hard enough that the panic in my chest escapes. I pull my little car blanket over my face and I start to cry.

As tears pour down my cheeks, I can't help but wonder: What was I thinking? I don't want this life. I don't want to worry about my privacy or Alex's. Our safety. I can't.

I thought it was worth it, but … no. I couldn't live with this fear day in and day out. I don't want a life where I'm constantly looking over my shoulder.

I peek out and find Alex on his phone. Alerting some sort of security maybe? Calling the police.

"There are pictures of us from karaoke and dancing. They're trying to figure out who you are to me." Alex turns to look at me. "Oh, darling." He tries to reach for my hand again, but I instinctively pull it away, back under the blanket. I'm collapsing in on myself and I can't let him suck me in again.

"Just get us out of here. I can't do this. I want to go to the hotel."

Hurt flashes across his face, but he nods. He begins inching forward and after several minutes we are away from them and on the way to the hotel.

"They're following us," Alex says.

"You can see them?" I wipe tears from my eyes.

"No. But they're there. They'll catch up quickly. They always do when they have something they're hunting."

"And they're hunting me, aren't they?" I feel sick. My stomach is in knots.

"It seems so, yes."

I sigh, then I sit silently, gripping the arm rests, until we are nearly at the hotel. All I can think about is how I need to get out of this situation. I need to feel safe again. I don't want to break his heart, and I certainly don't want to do it in a hurry while the paparazzi are rushing toward us, so I go ahead and rip off the bandage.

"I thought I could do this, but I can't."

"Ivy, please. It isn't always like this. I promise."

"But it happens. And I couldn't take the stress of it. Waiting for it to happen again. And now there are pictures of me all over the internet. *The mysterious woman Alexander Henry left Grey Blankenship for.* I can't tell you how much I hate that. I don't know what I've been thinking. Obviously, I haven't been. Not the past couple of days. I knew this wouldn't work. That we are from two very different worlds, but I let my heart take over, and it failed me." I take a deep breath and close my eyes when I notice the utter devastation on Alex's face. "You are truly fantastic. This has all to do with me and my fears, and what I want in my life." I gesture vaguely backward. "Stuff like this isn't welcome." My tears are flowing once again, sobs threatening to break free. Why is this the hardest thing I've ever done? *Maybe because I shouldn't,* some corner of my mind provides, without my permission.

"I can give it all up." He pulls to a stop outside the hotel.

"Alex. No. You cannot do that for me."

We stare at each other for a moment. Through my watery eyes, Alex looks at me so earnestly before making a confession.

"Ivy. I'm falling in love with you."

His words and his expression almost break me. But then I see a man with a huge camera moving toward the car. This was all much too fast. He thinks he loves me, but how could he possibly after a week? No, he would come to realize I'm not who he had made me out to be in his mind. He'll move on and be better for it.

"I don't think you are, Alex. Not really. We've been in a whirlwind of high emotions. You'll realize this is for the best." I have to run before the paparazzi swarm. "I'm sorry this is how it's ending." I unbuckled my seat belt and put my hand on the door before turning to Alex. His eyes are watery and there's a single tear running down his cheek. He looks like he wants to speak but can't overcome the lump in his throat.

"Goodbye, Alex."

For the second time, I leave Alex outside my hotel, not looking back. This time, though, it feels just like I knew it would. Devastating.

39

ALEXANDER

I FEEL HOLLOW. IF there were any doubt I'd truly fallen for Ivy, it's gone now. I wouldn't feel this way about someone who was only a passing interest.

I'm not sure of Ivy's exact itinerary, but I would imagine they are in Scotland by now. Part of me wants to drive up there and somehow find her. I got in the car three times yesterday, but never left the garage. If I got her to a place where she was wanting—even eager—to try to make something work, only to have her go back to her old doubts, I don't think I could bring her back.

I got a text from Mr. Crawley with what just so happened to be my final riddle, as I was watching Ivy walk into her hotel. I didn't look at it until this morning. It was an easy one. I think Aunt Agnes had lost steam once she got to the end. She'd sent me to the little theatre where I had played in *A Christmas Carol*. I went after breakfast, took the photo, sent it, and went straight home, where I got back in bed.

I didn't stay there long. It was useless. I proceeded to stare out the bedroom window at the overcast day. Everything was so grey and dull. It seemed fitting. I looked up the weather in Edinburgh, and it seems the weather is very similarly colored there today. I wonder if Ivy has drawn the same connection with the color and her feelings. Or maybe her feelings are more bright blue skies.

For some reason, though, I feel like she is likely as overcast as I am.

Now I'm standing in the solicitor's office, waiting to be called in.

"Mr. Crawley will see you now," the seemingly ancient woman at the front desk informs me.

I walk down the short hall and step into his office.

"Afternoon, Mr. Henry." He stands from his high-backed brown leather chair and walks toward a bookshelf.

"Good afternoon, Mr. Crawley."

"Have a seat," he says, jovially, as he pulls a large box from the top shelf. He brings it over and sets it in my lap. "Your box. You've earned it."

He circles back to his desk while I open the box. It's *not* filled with sandwich wrappers, nor was it any sort of joke. It's filled with old letters, what appears to be a series of journals and my grandfather's pocket watch. In the bottom, there are newspapers and some official-looking documents.

"Thank you," I tell the solicitor, then sigh. "I'm glad I came and did this." I'd been having very contrary feelings all morning. If I hadn't come, I wouldn't be feeling like my heart has been ripped out and thrown to the dogs. I'd been plagued by memories of her all evening and into the night. I'd taken a turn in mum's garden to get fresh air, only to see the ivy. I'd looked to the sky, only to have the constellations there remind me of the ones on her lovely face. I couldn't sit in the family room where we had watched that movie, and I certainly couldn't go to the pool.

Still, knowing what I know now, I'd do it again in a heartbeat. I told her when I suggested we pretend, that it would be worth a try, even if it didn't work out.

My feelings oscillate on whether that was true. Even so, I would do it again. I fear, though, she has ruined me for anyone else.

I have everything spread out on the dining room table when an idea strikes. This is my screenplay. This is what I want to do next. I have one more contracted film, but once I've fulfilled that obligation, I want to write about what I have here.

The box details my grandfather's time in World War II. He wrote about everywhere he went, and everything he did, with such great detail that, as I read, it feels like I'm living it alongside him. Every time he mentions writing, or receiving, a letter to my grandmother, I'm able to find the dated letter in the box. I see how my grandfather often downplayed the danger he was in, and my grandmother's encouragement, through what was obviously a difficult time for her as well. She'd taken a job at the old toy factory, repurposed in wartime to build tank engine components.

I spend hours reading the contents of the box, looking up events further in the book I purchased at the secondhand bookshop. Ivy's book had been in the bag with mine, and that set me back for a few minutes, but I compartmentalized and saved that sadness for another time. There was too much to look through, too much to think about and plan.

Before I am, once again, tempted to chase after Ivy, I text my assistant and ask him to arrange for my travel home. Or back to California. I now feel oddly confused about where home should be. You win, Aunt Agnes.

40

IVY

I'M STANDING, STARING UP at a castle on a cliff, and apart from being in Scotland, I have no idea where I am. A cool breeze makes me shiver, the sun's warmth absent on this dreary day.

"Anizey," Peter says, tugging on my jacket sleeve. "Do you think people live in there?"

I have no idea, but a quick look, beyond simply staring at the rock walls, gives me the answer. "No, buddy. There isn't a roof."

Peter, thankfully, doesn't seem to notice the flatness in my voice, but my sister does. Val moves over to stand beside me and sighs. "Remind me again why you had to leave Alexander."

"You know why, Val. I don't want to talk about it anymore."

When I got back to the hotel, I did my best to act like everything was fine. I wasn't ready to talk about it. Everyone could tell something was off with me, though. Even the kids walked around me on eggshells. Val and Micah let me be, thankfully, until we got on the train the next morning and I tried to hole myself up in my compartment. Val wasn't having that. She said we were going to talk and then I was going to enjoy the trip. We talked, but I wouldn't say I'm enjoying anything at the moment.

"I maintain that y'all could make it work. The best things aren't always the easiest or the most convenient."

"I know that. Believe me. But I don't want ... no. I'm not going through this with you again. And just because *I'm* mopey doesn't mean you shouldn't be enjoying your trip. I may not be fine right now, but I'll get there, so don't worry about me. Enjoy these ruins." I extend my arms toward the castle and give her the best smile I can manage.

"Fine. But I'm here for you anytime."

"Me too," Micah calls over, not looking our way.

My brother-in-law truly is the best. He'd been around while I was telling Val what had happened, and the only thing he contributed was that he would have gladly given up anything to be with Val. If Alex said he would give it all up for me, he might have been serious, and I shouldn't dismiss the offer out of some noble idea that I'm giving him what he actually wants.

His words almost had me reaching for my phone, until I remembered how it felt to be surrounded by the paparazzi. It's not that simple.

"I'm hungry," Juniper bounds over and informs us.

"Let's go find some lunch," Val says.

I bite into my scotch pie and know it should be delicious, but I can hardly taste it. It's the restaurant itself that brings me up and out of my cloud a bit. It's a seamless mix of old and new. So beautiful.

"I'm ready to get home to the restaurant. My contractor's emails have been very encouraging, but you know I'd rather be there overseeing things in person."

"The whole time leading up to the trip, I was sure you were gonna cancel on us and stay to see about the restaurant," Val says.

"I'll have you know that never crossed my mind. I did wish the timing was different, or you know, that the fire hadn't happened in the first place, but nothing was going to stop me from coming on this trip."

"But now you're ready to go back home? I don't think people on vacation usually say that," Juniper says before taking a huge bite of her chicken tender.

"Yeah. I want to stay forever," Peter adds. "Or go home but go to the beach."

"You've got to get home and back to swim team," Micah says.

"I can swim in the ocean." Peter shrugs.

They continue discussing swimming and vacations, and I'm not sure what else because I retreat into my brain, where I begin to stress. What if things aren't going as well in the restaurant as I think they are? I've been getting updates every other day with design items to choose, and vague updates about what they're working on.

It occurs to me that I might just be allowing myself to get stressed as some sort of twisted coping mechanism to deal with missing Alex. Should I do that?

I think I choose the stress.

"I'll be right back." Unable to eat any more, I leave my family at the table to go to the restroom. Not that I need to. I just want to move.

I'm looking down at the beautiful floor tiles as I walk, and bump right into someone very strong and sturdy. He's not wearing a kilt, but it's clear he's a local as soon as he opens his mouth.

He gets a hand underneath my elbow to keep me from bouncing off of him. "Whoa there, lassie. Ya nearly knocked me down." I look up and up, and find a gorgeous, ginger, bearded man. He's even taller than Alex. He smiles, and that in combination with his deep Scottish burr would have made me pass out a couple of weeks ago. I would have eyed him and said something about how there isn't a person on the earth who could knock him down. I would have engaged with him, been thrilled to talk with a local about what it's like to live in Scotland. I would have been so excited.

Not today.

"I'm sorry about that. I need to pay better attention."

He takes his hand from my elbow, waving off my apology. "Ah. An American. You've got a braw accent. From the southern part, I guess?"

My accent is braw? Good grief. "You are correct. I'm from North Carolina." Why did I offer that? I should be back on course to the restroom by now.

"North Carolina," he says with the beautiful rolling r's. "I'm Malcolm, by the way."

"Ivy." What am I doing? This man is captivating. Whoever ends up with him, I have a feeling, will be a lucky girl. But it's obviously not going to be me.

"Ivy. A bonnie name for a bonnie woman."

I smile and shake my head at him. "I could be married, you know."

"You're not wearing a ring. I checked."

"I could be seriously dating someone." Even saying that

makes me feel like garbage. Makes me wish I was. I'm so all over the place, and I don't like feeling like this. I can blame my upcoming period for some of this, but definitely not all of it.

"Are ye?"

"No. But I'm also not in the place to. I need to go. It was a pleasure meeting you, Malcolm."

"The pleasure was mine, darlin'."

Darlin'. Darling. Just like that, I burst into tears.

41

Alexander

Before my trip to London, I hardly used my home office, but in the three weeks since I've been back, I've been in there more than anywhere else. I flew through a pre-recorded screenwriting course, read everything my grandparents wrote, and I am now outlining a screenplay. I'm not going to be telling their story—I'm honestly not sure if they would want that—but I'm going to use it as a basic framework for a new story. Centered around the war, yes, but also centered around love. Love is the overarching theme of the box. It's what got my grandfather through his toughest days in the war, and the love and longing in their letters made me tear up more than once while reading. The tears likely had to do with my emotional state, because had I received this box without having met Ivy,

I'm not sure it would have made me cry.

At first, it was hard reading about their love after having lost mine. Their situation was obviously far more difficult, but still, the longing in their writing hit a little too close to home. However, their letters became more and more encouraging the longer I read. They had hope. They knew their love was strong and would survive until the war was over. If they could overcome and have the happy life I know they had, why couldn't Ivy and I?

I have a couple of months before filming is set to begin. We'll be filming for two months in Georgia. I'll be just over three and a half hours from Ivy, and I have a plan. If I can wait that long.

There was certainly damage control to be done when I got back from London. My agent drafted a statement reminding everyone that Grey and I had broken up just after the premiere of *The Mark of Everlore,* and we had never been engaged. I'd asked him to say that the woman in the photos was just a friend. He promptly pulled up the photos of us dancing and it was clear that would never work. I look like a man who is absolutely drowning in love for the woman in his arms. And one of the more encouraging things for me? She looks at me the very same way.

I'd hoped to keep her name out of the papers, but it was no use. I'd not been back in LA for fifteen minutes, when I got a message from my assistant that her name and her restaurant had been published all over. I'd wanted to text her. To grovel and apologize, but there was nothing I could say to make it better. Exactly what she'd feared had happened.

Instead, I issued a statement asking people to respect her privacy. Telling them that if they are looking for me, they will not find me with her, and that she does not lead a public life, and has no desire to.

I hope she saw it and read the apology between the lines.

~ele~

"You've got to get out of here and go ... literally anywhere," Grey says as she waltzes into my office.

"What are you doing here? I need to change the codes," I say, but I know I won't. Not because of Grey, anyway.

"We may not be in a fake relationship anymore, but we're still friends. You've been holed up in here like a hermit since you got back." She pauses, looking around at all the papers, letters, and journals, along with my empty take-out container from lunch. "And am I wrong?" She eyes me doubtfully.

Over a week of texts, I'd told her the abridged version of everything with Ivy. She'd always asked what I was up to, and looking back, I realize my answer was always the same. Working on something in my office.

"You're not wrong. But it's nothing to be concerned about.

I'm working on something exciting." I lean back in my desk chair. "People are going to think we're back together if you're letting yourself into my house."

"I was careful." She waved off my concern. "I'm glad you're working on something exciting, but what about Ivy? How is your heart?"

"How is my heart?" I laugh at her phrasing. "It's been better, but I've decided not to give up."

"Good. I'm *so* glad to hear that. It can work out. I know it can."

"Aren't you still seeing your boyfriend from back home in secret? How often do you see each other?" If anyone could understand my situation, it's Grey.

"Yes, I'm still seeing Conner. We see each other once a month or so, depending on filming. Sometimes more than that." She shrugs as if this is fine. Perfectly normal. Like it's something I could do and be happy with.

I am not like Grey.

"That sounds terrible."

"It works for now. It's not permanent. He has to stay home because he's his grandfather's caregiver. But one day ... one *sad* day, his grandfather will no longer be with us, and Conner will come out here. We'll get married, and he will be my trophy husband." She grins at that last bit.

"And he will be content to just bum about at home? And be

your arm candy?"

"Arm candy? Always. I'm sure eventually he would want to get a job of some sort, but honestly, he has worked so hard these past several years, that I wouldn't blame him if he never worked another day in his life."

One major difference with my situation is that Ivy would never want to live here. I certainly can't imagine her wanting to bum about too much. She loves her job and her small-town life.

"You seem lost in your thoughts. Please tell me you're cooking up a plan to get your girl back."

I smile. Grey really is a good friend. "I'm making alterations to a plan, yes."

"How can I help?"

Mr. and Mrs. Parker are standing behind their restaurant counter, heads bent together, looking at a paper. Mr. Parker has his arm around his wife, and it makes me smile.

"Good morning," I say as I approach.

"Ah, Alexander. Wonderful to see you," Mr Parker says, and I try my best to store their warm smiles in a permanent space in my memory.

"I'm glad to see you both, as well. And I'd love it if you

would call me Alex. I've always preferred that name. I'm not sure why I've always given Alexander to people." I don't know why I ask this of them given what I've come here to tell them. I think I've got used to Ivy calling me Alex, and I miss it. Maybe that's the name I want those I care for most to call me.

This request makes Mrs. Parker grin like she knows why I asked.

"What can we get you today, Alex?" she asks, and for a moment, I can see how mum-like she is, and it makes me miss having one. Mine was, in many ways, quite different from Mrs. Parker, but the tenderness and the urge to care for others are the same.

"I always love it when you surprise me."

"I know just the thing. Have a seat and I'll pop by with your tea and water in a minute."

"Would you both have a moment to sit and talk with me?"

"Sure," Mr. Parker says. "Maybe I'll have some tea, too."

"Have you tried the hot tea before?" I ask, wondering if I should confess and warn him off.

"I have. It's a nice change from coffee sometimes."

I nod. Maybe I'm a tea snob. I head to my usual booth and wait.

A couple of minutes later, they are seated across from me, each of us with a tea and a blueberry muffin.

"What's going on, Alex, dear?" Mrs. Parker says without

preamble.

"I came in today because it's been a while and I wanted to see you. And also because I wanted to let you know that I may not be around much anymore."

"Got a big film to shoot somewhere far away?" Mr. Parker asks.

My eyes go wide, and they both laugh.

"Teddy and I may not watch television or films," Mrs. Parker says with a smile, "but we're not totally unaware. We just see you as a person, like anyone else, so that's how we treated you at first. Then you became more than just a person to us. You slowly became like family. Family we don't often get to see. But family, nonetheless." She reaches across the table and pats my hand.

"Also," Mr. Parker added. "We don't *usually* watch TV or movies, but we went to see *The Mark of Everlore*."

Mrs. Parker smiled. "We wanted to support you and see you at work."

"You went to see it? Really?"

"Really. And we are so proud of you," Mrs. Parker said. "It was wonderful."

Mr. Parker nodded.

"I can't tell you how much that means to me. And I'm sorry I never told you. At first, I really enjoyed being with people who didn't know. Which apparently wasn't the case.

And then, as time went on, it felt like a weird thing to come out and say."

"We understood why you never said anything. You were genuine in all the ways that matter, and that's all we needed, to know you were special to us," Mr. Parker said, clapping a hand on my shoulder from across the table.

"And not in the way you're special to the world," Mrs Parker adds. "I know you don't have any family left on this earth, but I want you to know that you have us."

Tears fill my eyes. I've never been much of a crier, but here I am, yet again, letting my emotions have full reign. Mrs. Parker urges her husband out of the booth, then slides out. Before I know it she's sitting beside me, pulling me into her arms.

It's probably a full minute before she relaxes her arms and straightens. "Alright. Tell us about this movie that's stealing you away."

I smile. "It's not a movie. I mean, there is one before long. But the thing is ... I've met someone."

42

IVY

I don't know how my contractor has managed to do all he has in such a short amount of time, but here we are—not even a month after returning from our trip—and the restaurant is nearly ready to reopen. It's like he had an army in here working while I was gone. And I cannot describe how shocked I was walking in after we got home. The place was stunning. And it's come together even more in the past few weeks.

It's exactly like I wanted. Better, really. It looks as if it were professionally designed, not pieced together by someone on vacation, and a contractor who's been wearing what appears to be decades-old work clothes every time I've seen him.

However this has been accomplished, it's a dream. The perfect representation of the past, with just enough modern touches to be stylish and practical. I love it.

"Anizey, I'm tired of carrying things up the stairs."

"You've made three trips, Peter." I shake my head, smiling down at my nephew. "And I thought you were an athlete."

He and Juniper had protested hard when, three days ago, I had let the family know that I was going to be moving back into my apartment. I think maybe this is his last-ditch effort to keep me around.

"Buddy, you can come visit me anytime."

"It's not the same. And what about breakfast? Yours is so much better."

I'd begun cooking family breakfast when we got home from England. It gave me a reason to get up and moving. I wasn't really needed at the restaurant, although I went every day. I much prefer making decisions in person, not that there was much deciding to be done at that point.

"Who says I'll *never* be at breakfast? And you all can come here and eat anytime. Just tell your mom to let me know."

"Fine." He took his not terribly heavy-looking box and headed up the stairs.

I would miss being with my family, but I was very excited to get back to my apartment. The restaurant wasn't the only thing now more beautiful. My place only needed painting and new flooring, but the updates really made a difference. I went shopping yesterday for new curtains and bedding. It is going to be my little cozy retreat.

I'm heading toward the back to get another box from the back of Val's minivan when there's a knock on the restaurant's door. A man is standing there holding a large cardboard box. I run to let him in. As I unlock the door, I look across the street and find two paparazzi still lingering, hoping to spot Alex, or the two of us together. When I first came to the restaurant after arriving back home, there had been twelve out there. I guess they're slowly catching on to the fact that Alex isn't around and won't be. There isn't a story here.

"Delivery for Ivy Hawkins."

"That's me." Curious, I'm not expecting anything. Probably something the contractor ordered.

"Good thing you're here; this is supposed to stay temperature controlled."

Curiouser.

He set the box on a table near the door. "If you'll sign here, I'll be on my way," the man said cheerily.

I scrawl my signature on his tablet, thank him, grab the box, and run to the back.

No time to waste when you've got a mystery box of possibly perishable goods.

I run a knife along the tape and pop the box open. Inside is a styrofoam cooler completely filled with Crunchies.

"Alex," I whisper, then sigh. I unwrap a Crunchie and take

a bite while collapsing onto a stool.

"Ivy! We're not carrying all your stuff upstairs without you!" Val rushes into the kitchen like she's been looking for me.

"I got a delivery." I take another sadly delicious bite.

"What in the world?" she says, looking into the box. "Did you order these?"

"Nope. Alex said he was going to send me a bunch to sell in the restaurant. I assumed he wouldn't, or that he'd forgotten."

"Guess he's the kind of guy who does what he says he's gonna do."

"Yeah." He really is. He's someone I could trust, and I left him.

"Man. I wonder how many are in here."

I shrug. "You should have one. They're delicious."

Val pulls one out of the box and begins unwrapping it. "So how are you feeling?"

"Not great."

"This is so good," Val says through a bite. "Sorry you're not feeling great. Wanna talk about it?"

"I miss him. I've been keeping myself so busy so I wouldn't think about him, but I keep thinking of things I want to tell him. Or having random memories."

"But having evidence of *him* thinking of *you* is harder, I imagine." Val takes another bite.

"Yes. He's so thoughtful and so kind. And I trust him. You

know that's a big deal for me."

"I know."

"I didn't realize how much I trusted him until now. I mean, he had to have ordered this recently, right? We've been home awhile. So he remembered what he told me, and even though I did what I did, he did what he said he would. But I know I trusted him before. He never gave me a reason not to." I stand and begin pacing around the kitchen.

"You didn't trust him when he told you he would give things up for you."

"I believed he would. I just didn't want him to have to."

"Maybe he had weighed the cost and knew it was worth it. He told you he loved you."

"He did."

"I bet he still does."

"After how I rejected him and left? You should have seen his face. I think I broke him too much for him to still want to be with me." I stop by the box and unwrap a second Crunchie. "Maybe I made a mistake. But it's too late."

43

Alexander

ALEX

> I don't want that role. I have other things I want to focus on.

I shouldn't be surprised when my phone lights up with my agent's name.

"Hey, Isaac."

"Starring in that movie will catapult you into a stardom the likes of which the world has never seen. You have to do it."

"I don't want stardom the likes of which the world has never seen. Whatever that means. And like I said, I have other things I'm focused on in my career and my personal life."

I hear him sigh over the phone. "You're sure? I have to let

them know tomorrow."

"I'm sure."

He sounds a bit defeated when he speaks. "Well, what is this you're working on for your career? Can I help in any way?"

I fill him in on my project and we make a rough plan. It feels good to have him in on my screenplay. He may get overenthusiastic about things, like wanting me to take that role, but he's a great agent.

I end the call and find a text waiting from Mrs. Parker.

REBECCA PARKER

> We decided to close the restaurant.

I call her.

"Hello?"

"You can't just drop that sort of news in a text."

"Hello, Alex. How are you, dear?"

I grin. "I'm sorry. I'm doing very well. I hope you both are."

"We are. We're excited. Do you know how difficult it is to take a vacation or even just relax when you own and operate a restaurant?"

I hear Mr. Parker in the background. "I've told her for years we need to hire a manager."

"I couldn't trust anyone else to do things the way I want. But anyway, this Saturday is our last day. And we already have two prospective buyers. Apparently, we are in a highly desirable location."

I'm hit with a crazy idea. "Would you like to take a trip with me? I'm going to North Carolina next week. I'd like your opinion on something."

"To see Ivy? My opinion is yes!"

I laugh. "Your opinion on Ivy or your opinion on going?"

"Both."

"Alright." I chuckle. "I want your opinion on something I'm considering buying. I'm coming to eat later, and I'll fill you in."

⸻ ello ⸻

"Alex, this is too much." This was at least the fourth time Mrs. Parker has said something of that nature. She's taking her seat beside me in first class, with Mr. Parker just across the aisle. I'd asked her to sit with me to avoid sitting with a stranger.

"Not for you, it's not," I remind her. They had become my family without me realizing it, and I was going to treat them to anything they'd let me.

"I think this seat is more comfortable than my recliner," Mr. Parker says with a laugh.

We're on the red-eye, so once the flight is at altitude and

everyone is settled, the cabin lights dim. I'm happy to see both Parkers asleep within minutes. Did they take something? I didn't think it was possible to fall asleep so quickly on a plane.

I'm sure I won't sleep at all, until five minutes later when I'm startled awake by an announcement stating we will be beginning our descent into Charlotte. I guess I did sleep, and sleep hard.

"There you are," Mrs. Parker says. "I was afraid you'd be too excited to sleep."

"I was too."

"Have any particularly pleasant dreams?" she asks with a grin and raised eyebrows.

"Not that I know of, but I'm heading toward one. At least I hope I am."

Mrs. Parker places her hand on my knee. "She'd be a fool not to see you and jump right into your arms."

We're met by a car at a discreet exit for high-profile passengers, then I drive us west. Mountains come into view in the distance as we near Ivy's town. It's peaceful out here. Certainly different from the places I've lived. I can see why she likes it.

I pull out my phone and aim it at my face to unlock it, then hand it to Mrs. Parker. "Will you text Micah and tell him we will be there in five minutes?"

"Sure."

Minutes later, we pull in front of a white farmhouse with a

wraparound porch, surrounded by huge trees. Micah is running a few minutes behind us, so we hop out and walk around outside, eager to stretch our legs. We walk through a gate into the backyard, where we find a pool surrounded by beautiful, almost tropical-looking plants. It reminds me of my mum's plants around our pool in London.

"Hey, Alexander!" Micah calls as he steps into the backyard.

"Micah! Good to see you." I walk toward him and shake his hand, then make introductions.

"It's hot out. Let's get inside," Micah suggests.

"Lead the way."

Ivy's restaurant opens tomorrow, and it's torture being in her town without seeing her, but I really want to surprise her at the opening.

I want to tour the town, but instead, the Parkers and I have visited everywhere within a half-hour drive. I need a distraction today, though. My patience has worn thin.

"Remember that sign we saw for tubing in Saluda? We could go do that," I suggest, sitting down in a chair in the Parkers' room in our bed and breakfast.

"We didn't bring swimsuits. And I'm not sure tubing is for us. We aren't athletes."

I eye the couple who have spent their adult lives on their feet moving around within their restaurant. They may not be athletes, but they're plenty spry.

"I'm pretty sure tubing is for anyone who can get in a tube and swim if needed. It's not rapids, just a gentle float."

We stop at my first ever Walmart and buy swimwear. I smile, remembering Ivy teasing me and my five-pack of underwear in that store near Dover. She'd have something to say about my palm-frond-covered swimming trunks.

I wear sunglasses and a hat. To my knowledge I'm not recognized once as I float down the Green River in a tube tied to Mrs. Parker. Mr. Parker is on her other side. There are plenty of people on the water, but it doesn't feel crowded. I'm filled with peace as I lie on my back and watch the sky and trees pass by.

Tomorrow will be good. Tomorrow will change my life. I'm going to hold my future in my arms.

"Alex," Mrs. Parker says.

"Hmm?"

"I think you should call us something other than Mr. and Mrs. Parker."

I turn my head toward them both and I speak words, not really knowing they're coming out of my mouth. "You could go ahead and choose grandparent names; you'll need them eventually."

I can tell Granny Parker wants to tackle me in a hug but doesn't want to take a dive into the water, so I reach over and squeeze her hand.

"I've got some good ideas," she says, and her husband grins.

44

IVY

I'M DOING A FINAL restaurant walkthrough with the contractor, and everything looks like a dream. It's so much more than I could have ever imagined.

"Tom. This is ..." I shake my head, not knowing how to reply. "Thank you."

He waved me off. "We did quality work, but I think it was the decorator that made it look so great. I'm going to have to try to work with her again." Tom said that last part mostly to himself.

"What decorator?" I ask, then watch as the color drains from Tom's typically rosy cheeks.

He doesn't answer.

"You never mentioned a decorator. And I know I didn't *pay*

for a decorator. What's going on, Tom?"

"I wasn't supposed to say."

I turn to face Tom fully. "Well, you have to now."

"While you were in England, I was contacted by a man who said he had extra money to put into the project. He wanted to pay for a decorator, and he wanted me to hire extra workers so the project would move faster."

"So all the emails you sent with options and things for me to approve were things from the decorator?"

"Yes."

"And the only reason we're ready to open so much sooner—"

"Yes."

I am flabbergasted. "Was the person's name Alexander?"

"No. His name was Mark."

Mark. That must be Alex's assistant. I'm about ten percent mad that Alex did this, but then I look around with fresh eyes at the gift he gave me. And then think about the income from opening early and being able to get my employees back to work. Surprisingly, most of them waited for us to reopen rather than getting other jobs. I'd been so relieved for them when it was clear they would get to come back sooner.

All thanks to Alex.

"I'm sorry about keeping this from you, Miss Hawkins. I was afraid if I said anything, the money would be gone, and I really wanted this to be the best it could be. And to be able to get you back open as soon as I could."

"It's fine, Tom. I'm glad I know now, though. I'm just grateful to be ready to open this beautiful restaurant."

"Me too. I'm ready for one of your breakfast bowls."

I smile. "Come for breakfast tomorrow. It's on the house."

"Na uh," Val says, a forkful of spaghetti paused on the way to her mouth. I'm at Val and Micah's dining room table having supper with my family.

"He's the only reason I'm able to open tomorrow."

"And that it's so gorgeous. Man. Is his assistant like a private investigator?" Val finally takes her bite.

"I don't think it would be terribly hard to figure this out. The location of my restaurant would be a simple Google search, and Tom is one of only two contractors in the area." I take a sip of my water, unable to eat. The missing of Alex and feeling like I've made a huge mistake have my stomach churning.

"Still. And to have the audacity to hire a designer behind your back for your restaurant? Why did he think that would be okay?" Val sets down her fork.

"I had told him my vision, and Tom emailed me options and

had me approve everything. I'm not upset about it."

Val's gaze slides to her husband. "You're being suspiciously quiet."

Micah looked at Val for a moment, then turned his gaze to me. "I'm glad you're not mad. I helped coordinate things and approved the designer's idea."

"Micah!" Val yells.

"Dad's in trouble." Peter laughs, and Juniper joins him.

"He wanted it to be a surprise. He told me about their plan to communicate with Ivy about the design, that it would be something she would love."

Honestly, I'm not upset. Should Micah have told me, or stopped it in the first place? Yes? No? I don't know. I'm happy with how everything turned out. The only unsettling thing is, once again, the feeling of possibly making a mistake by leaving him.

"Guys, it's fine. Everything turned out for the best. I'm sorry to leave y'all with the dishes, but I think I need to go on. The morning's gonna come early."

"What time are you getting up?" Juniper asks.

"I have to get up by five to have time to get ready and get down to the kitchen to have everything ready to open at seven." I have two kitchen staff who will be there at five-thirty, and three servers arriving at six-thirty. It may be overkill for the early breakfast crowd, but I'd rather be prepared in case people are excited for the reopening. I've been all over social media, hyping it up. I'm so excited to be back in business.

I'm so far out of the habit of getting up early, that the walk from the bed to the bathroom feels like I've been covered in mud and wrapped in weighted blankets. I showered last night and did my curly hair routine, complete with the new addition of sleeping in a bonnet. I love how smooth my curls are now in the mornings. They're still wild by the end of the day with the humidity here, but I'll take what I can get.

I make quick work of getting ready, wearing my cutest working-hard-but-also-talking-to-customers outfit. I chose jeans and a sheer black top covered in tiny white hearts over a tank, complete with red flats that are nearly as comfortable as sneakers.

I head down to the kitchen, make a pot of coffee, and start the grits—they have to cook the longest. I'm cracking eggs as my kitchen staff arrive and I'm surrounded by the familiar kitchen bustle that I love. It isn't long before the servers step into the kitchen. I'm taking a moment to sit on a stool and sip my coffee, and I grin when they walk in.

"Welcome back," I say to the two girls, Tilly and Jess, who've worked here since I opened. "And welcome," I add, to the man

I hired last week."

"It's so good to be back," the girls say in unison, and we all laugh.

"I'm gonna check on things out front," I say, standing from my stool.

"No. You relax and enjoy your coffee. Everything is perfect out there. We're ready," Tilly says.

"But you should come out to flip the sign and unlock the door when it's time," Jess adds.

I relax back onto my stool, deciding to trust them—and myself, because I was just out there last night—and enjoy the last few minutes of relative peace.

Twenty minutes later, I step onto the restaurant floor and head to the door to officially open, when I notice two things at once and gasp. Small vases filled with peonies in pinks and corals on all the tables, and my first customer is somehow already inside, sitting with his back to me. He must have heard my intake of breath because he straightens, then he stands. When he turns, I stop breathing.

"Hello, darling."

45

Alexander

It hadn't occurred to me to be nervous. A bit anxious and excited, yes, but I'd been busy enacting my plan. Now, though, as I watch Ivy, looking as stunning as ever, she stares at me, and I see the cogs turning in her mind. I'm nervous. Why is it I expected her to feel differently than when she left me in London? Distance doesn't always make the heart grow fonder. What can I say to show her I meant it when I said I would give things up for her?

"I bought—" I begin, but my words seem to have woken her and she's running toward me. She jumps into my arms so hard and so fast that I have to take two steps back to avoid us becoming better acquainted with the floor. "—a house here."

"You're here!" she says into my ear, as her cheek presses

against mine. Then she leans back to look into my eyes. "And you … what?"

"I bought a house here."

"Why? I mean, really?" She puts her feet on the floor but keeps her arms around my neck. I pull her to me.

"There is no place I'd rather be. I have one more film I'm contracted to be in, but after that, we'll figure it out."

"We'll figure it out," she repeats breathlessly.

I look over Ivy's shoulder where the restaurant staff, her family, and the Parkers stand. "I want to kiss you, but we have an audience."

She didn't even glance their way. "I don't care if you don't." She tilted her chin up toward me, and I meet her the rest of the way. As soon as our lips touch, it's coming home. It's right. It's good. It's everything I could ever want. It's rain on dry land.

Ivy threads her fingers through my hair, and I pick her up again. Claps and cheers fill the air, and I feel Ivy smile against my lips before she speaks. "Maybe we need to wait for a more private moment to have a proper hello."

I loosen my hold on her, so she slides slowly down my body. "I like the sound of that." Before we go visit the crowd, I cup her face in my hands. "I don't know when I've ever been so happy." I lean down and kiss her forehead, then stay close, keeping my words soft. Just for us. "I love you, darling."

"You do?" she whispers, almost as if she can't believe it.

"I do. I know it's fast, but that doesn't make it untrue. And I certainly don't expect—"

"I think ..." she interrupts, then takes a slow breath. "I think I love you too."

My heart absolutely pounds in my chest with the need to kiss her again, heedless of our audience. I bring her lips back to mine, then wrap my arms around her. She moans softly against my lips as she squeezes me tighter. It takes all my willpower to keep from picking her up and carrying her somewhere more private.

Instead, I dip Ivy low like we're dancing, not breaking the kiss. The crowd roars again, and it's enough to bring us out of our little bubble. I bring her upright once more and say, "I've got some people for you to meet, then I want to try your grits."

The Parkers are, as I knew they would be, completely smitten with Ivy, and the feeling is entirely mutual. Ivy gave them a tour of the kitchen until patrons began trickling in. When she asked us what we wanted to eat, Mrs. Parker told her to surprise us, then winked at me.

We took a seat in the booth closest to the kitchens, because I wanted to have the best chance to glimpse Ivy as often as possible. Surprising her at the opening sounded all well and good until it was time for her to get to work.

She brings out coffees for the Parkers and tea for me. It's prepared just how I like it. She was paying attention.

It isn't long before she arrives with our breakfast. "I brought you each my current favorite," she said, setting a bowl in front of each of us. "It's grits with scrambled eggs, and a sweet potato, bacon, and kale hash. And a bowl of bread," she adds, setting a bowl of cloth-wrapped bread in the center of the table.

Mrs. Parker peels back the cloth. "Biscuits and muffins!"

"Yep," Ivy says with a grin.

"Are they blueberry?" Mr. Parker asks.

"They are. We have other flavors at times, but these are a staple."

Mr. Parker grins. "I love blueberry muffins."

"I love this place. I haven't eaten a bite, but I already love it," Mrs. Parker says, picking up her fork.

The look on Ivy's face is so pleased, so ecstatically happy. She loves what she has done here, and now I can fully understand why she didn't want to leave it.

"I love it too," I say. "This place is amazing. Is it odd to say that I'm proud of you?"

She grins and bends to kiss my cheek. "Nope." She straightens. "I wanna see you try your grits before I get back to work."

"It's a bit scary to try something with an audience," I say, then push my eggs aside to get to the grits underneath. I watch Ivy as I bring my fork to my mouth, her clear green eyes never leave mine as I take my bite.

Delicious. Smooth and creamy. Just the right amount of saltiness.

"I had no idea what I was missing."

A grin spread across Ivy's face. "I knew you'd like them!" Her response is loud, drawing the attention of everyone nearby. The Parker's laugh.

"This is all absolutely delicious," Mrs. Parker says, using her fork to point to her bowl.

Mr. Parker nods as he takes a second bite of his muffin.

"Thank you," Ivy says. "I'm so happy y'all are here." She eyes me particularly, and I swear, my heart sprouts wings and floats around in my chest.

She goes back to work, and I see her moving through the kitchen three times before she's out again, winking at me as she passes our table. I see her four times before she is out again, and squeezes my shoulder as she passes by. I'm staring toward the kitchen when Mrs. Parker clears her throat.

"I think we've sat here long enough. There are people waiting."

I look over my shoulder and, sure enough, the restaurant is full and there are several people waiting around the hostess stand near the door.

I give Mr. Parker my credit card. "I'm sure Ivy won't let us pay, but I want to. Will you take care of it while I tell her goodbye?"

He salutes, and I take off toward the kitchen with a smile.

46

IVY

I'M SCATTERING GRILLED PEPPERS on top of a bowl when the kitchen goes silent. Alex must have stepped in here. The staff have been beside themselves all morning. I was afraid it would negatively affect our efficiency, but if anything, it's helped.

Alex's arms wrap around me before I have the chance to turn. I set down the food, take off my gloves, and back us up from the food prep area. He places a kiss on my neck and holds me tighter.

"When will you finish up here?" he asks, nuzzling into the side of my face.

"We close at two, and I'll likely be finished by three."

"Can I pick you up then and take you somewhere to rub

your feet, and feed you?" He turns me around to face him, keeping his arms firmly around me. "And kiss you like I really want to."

Thankfully, he's keeping his voice low, but the kitchen staff are openly staring. It's too late to care at this point. I slide my hands up his chest, and around his neck as I go up on my toes and press my lips to his.

"As long as the kissing can be first," I say against his lips.

"Hmmm ... we'll see how things go."

I push against his chest and smile.

"Fine, the kissing can be first. Whatever you want, darling."

"I like the sound of that," I say. "Now get out of here. You're so distracting."

He pulls me to him and kisses my cheek. "Fine. But I'll be counting down the minutes until three."

When Alex left, I thought time was going to drag, but I got in the zone. I enjoyed putting bowls together and greeting my regulars—including Fran Randolph and her Bible verses. Before I knew it, the restaurant was closed, and we were cleaning and preparing for tomorrow.

Alex came in through the back entrance at three o'clock on the dot. He leaned against the kitchen doorframe, arms crossed, watching me double-check everything was turned off and ready for tomorrow. As soon as I locked the door, he took my hand and led me to the passenger seat of his SUV, which, come to find out, is not a rental.

He drives me ten minutes down the road to a beautiful white farmhouse. I imagine sitting in a rocking chair, drinking lemonade on the porch. A picnic table under the trees. Alex opens my door for me—because he insists I wait for him to do that—and he takes my hand and leads me toward the house.

He pulls his keys from his pocket as we step onto the porch, and he unlocks and opens the door. "Welcome to my new home."

We step inside, and I'm greeted by a beautiful old staircase, and what looks like well-kept original wood floors.

"I can't believe you bought a house. Here." My eyes are wide as I take in all the beautiful character that's been preserved. It has arched doorways. Arched doorways!

"I know there is more for us. Trust me when I say this is absolutely what I want."

"I trust you." He gives my hand a little squeeze because he knows the gravity of those words. "And I love it."

"It needs a little work."

"Well, you know a good contractor." I raise my eyebrows, and he narrows his eyes at me. "Tom accidentally spilled the beans a couple of days ago."

He nods. "So … were you … upset? Or … happy?"

"I landed on happy, although I'm not sure what I was going to do about it. Then you showed up, and I think I'll just show you how happy I am."

"Oh really?" His grin is as wide as I've ever seen it. "I didn't do it for any sort of reward. But I think I'd like to collect. What are you thinking?" He pushes his glasses up the bridge of his nose.

I put my hands on his chest and push him until his legs hit the sofa, which appears to be the only piece of furniture in the house, then I push him down.

"I'm quite enjoying this so far," Alex says. Something about his voice and accent hits my ears just right, making me shiver. I climb onto his lap, and his smile disappears as he gazes at me intensely.

I take his face in my hands and place a soft kiss on his lips. "Thank you, Alex," I whisper against his lips, where I stay as I slide my hand back into his hair.

He wraps his arms around me and tugs me closer. "Have I told you I quite fancy you?"

I lean my head back to catch his beautiful blue eyes with mine. "You've mentioned it."

"If you don't hear it from me a million more times before this life is over, I will have failed."

I bring my lips back to his for a moment, that turns to

minutes, that turns to I don't know how long, then I whisper in my best English accent, "I quite fancy you too."

He throws his head back in a laugh, then brings his hands to my face, his fingertips playing softly in my hair. "I love you, darling."

I sigh. "I love it when you call me darling. Honestly, I think when you started that ... that's when I started being unable to fight the pull toward you."

He puts his arms back around me and gives me what can only be described as a sassy look. "For me, it was seeing you in your new dresses for the first time."

"Be serious!" I swat his arm and smile.

"I truly don't know. My feelings came hard and fast, but they were also a slow build. I knew when I met you, you were someone special. I knew at the pool that I was desperate for more of you. I knew on the gondola that I wanted to try with you, that the pretend thing wasn't working for me and never had. And when you sang karaoke, I knew that I would stay with you, no matter what it took, for as long as you'd let me."

"Alex, I never wanted you to have to give anything up, and it looks like that's exactly what's happening. And all I've done is gain."

"I'd been itching for a change for a while. I did what I wanted to in Hollywood, and now I'm over it. I don't long for fame or money. I still want to create, but I have a plan for that. It all starts with the box."

"Oh my gosh! I forgot about the box. What was in it?" I move off Alex's lap to sit beside him, and he pouts.

"It was full of my grandfather's World War II things and letters he exchanged with my grandmother."

"Wow. I can't wait to see it all."

"I wish I had brought it with me." Alex twirls one of my curls around his finger. "I'm writing a screenplay. A love story set in World War II. And the good thing about screenplay writing is I can do it anywhere. I mean, I'll have to travel some, but mostly, I could be here."

I launch myself at Alex and pin him to the sofa. I kiss him until I hear something and turn to find the Parkers standing there with shopping bags.

Did they buy throw pillows?

47

ALEXANDER

I've been back with Ivy for three days now. I've been staying at a bed and breakfast, but the bed was too short for me, so the first piece of furniture—after the sofa—that I want to buy, is a bed.

"Lie down and see what you think," I tell Ivy, as we stand in the middle of a sea of mattresses, looking at one that claims to be perfect for most sleep types.

"It doesn't matter what I think."

"It will."

She raises her eyebrows at me. "That's presumptuous."

"We'll be married before too long."

"Will we now?"

I lean down and whisper into her ear. "When I know what I

want, I'm not afraid to go for it. And my sole focus right now is securing a lifetime with you."

Ivy shivers, and I place a kiss on her temple, then place my hand on the small of her back, urging her toward the bed.

From that point forward, our shopping experience is a blur because I can't get thoughts of rings, weddings, and everything with Ivy, out of my mind. I don't know anything about the mattress I buy, apart from the fact that Ivy likes it. And it's the same with the bed frame. It could have unicorns on it, and I wouldn't know. Mentally, I'm at a jewelry shop.

I need to refocus. She deserves my full attention.

I thread my fingers through Ivy's and kiss her cheek when we step out of the store, heading to the car and then on to dinner.

"Tell me more about your screenplay," she requests as she fastens her seatbelt.

"It's about this woman named Ivy—"

She shoves my shoulder. "No, it's not."

I chuckle. "No. I haven't yet named the female lead. I've just been calling her Jane."

"And you don't want to use your grandparents' names?"

"No. I want to honor them, but not use their actual story or their names." I turn out of the car park toward the restaurant.

"I love that. Will I get to read it when you're finished?"

"I was hoping you would. It's a little nerve-wracking doing something new like this. Obviously, I'm very familiar with screenplays, but I don't yet know if writing one will be outside of my skill set."

"I'm betting you'll do well with it," Ivy says with a confident smile.

"I'm not sure that confidence is warranted, but thank you, darling."

She shrugs and leans over the console, lying her head on my shoulder.

⸻ ←← ⸻

"Have you ever been here?" I ask. I wanted to surprise her, but it's hard to know where she has and has not been in the area surrounding her town.

"I haven't. Actually, I don't remember ever seeing it. It looks kinda new to me."

I smile as our server approaches and hands us menus. He's an older man, and his wrinkled face turns surprised when he sees me.

"Alexander Henry. Well, I'll be."

I look down and see he is wearing a nametag. "Walter. Well, I'll be."

He claps me on the shoulder and chuckles. "What can I get you two to drink?" He removes his hand and pulls his pen from his shirt pocket.

"I'll have a sweet tea," I answer. "Ivy?"

"Make that two. With lemon." She smiles up at Walter, who meticulously writes down our drink order before turning to go. "Going for the full southern experience with the tea?"

"I hear y'all make fantastic sweet tea," I say with my, and I'm not bragging, nearly perfect Southern accent.

Ivy's jaw drops. "Why have you never done that for me before?"

"Have you not seen *Time Under the Willow*? I played a man from Georgia."

"Oh." She pauses to think. "I guess you did. I'd forgotten."

I laugh and take Ivy's hand across the table.

She smiles and the love in her eyes is almost overwhelming.

She looks down at her menu. "They have fish and chips!"

"That's why we're here. I hunted all western North Carolina for fish and chips, and this was the closest place. I know you had gotten tired of eating it, so you could certainly get something else, but I thought maybe enough time had passed."

"I think I'm ready. The problem is, now that I've had the real thing, I'm worried this will be a disappointment."

"We can get you something else if it is."

Walter comes back with our teas and takes our order. I get a burger I think she'll like, just in case.

Ivy sips her tea. "Mmmm. I need to see what kind of tea bags they use or how they do it because this is amazing. I've been thinking the tea at Bowl could improve."

"I'll ask," I say, and a look of gratitude well beyond me asking about the tea covers her face. "What's going on?"

"It's just ..." Ivy sighs. "When I decided I wanted to try to date, I wanted to find someone to be my partner. In life, of course, but also to help me with restaurant things when needed. I was feeling overwhelmed with the fire and remodel, but running a restaurant is hard. I'm up for the challenge, but it would be nice to not always be doing everything myself." Her eyes swim with tears.

I reach across the table and take her face in my hands. "Ivy, I'm here for you always. Whatever you need. However I can help."

She turns her head and kisses my palm. "I love you, Alex."

"Darling ..." I lean across the table and kiss the love of my life. "You are the unexpected gift I didn't realize I needed, and love isn't a big enough word for how I feel about you."

Walter returns with our food and wordlessly sits it in front of us.

Ivy looks down at her plate. "It doesn't look the same."

"It may taste just as good."

"It may."

I lean over the table and kiss her briefly. "Say the word and I'll take you back to England. Whenever you want."

"Oh yeah? She smiles. "Is this offer valid indefinitely?"

"Forever," I say.

And then she says words that are as unexpected as they are elating. "Let's get married."

"What? Are you ... serious?"

"Why wait? It would be quick, but I don't have any doubts. Not anymore."

I look into her beautiful green eyes for a moment, searching for any sense of doubt. There is none. "It will be my incredible honor to be your husband, Ivy."

"Good. That's settled," she says, eyes sparkling, then in her English accent adds, "I'm looking forward to forever, darling."

EPILOGUE

IVY--THREE YEARS LATER

"What are you doing here? You just had a baby. I was gonna send something over to you in a bit," Rebecca Parker says as she scoops my toddler into her arms and kisses his cheek. "Good morning, Ben. How are you today?"

"I'm tired, Nana. Mummy woke me up too early and said we were gonna get breakus." He rubs his black curly hair against his nana's neck and closes his eyes. He calls me Mummy, and it's the most wonderful thing I have ever heard.

"I wanted a bowl, and I haven't been out of the house in four days. Alex is smothering me. We had to get out before he woke up. I'd forgotten what he was like when Ben was born, and I swear he is twice as bad this time." I sit at the nearest table, and Rebecca reaches out with her free hand to gently touch the baby's bald head where it pokes out from behind the fabric that straps her to me.

Teddy Parker's voice booms as he walks from the back. "Well, I thought I heard my babies were in here." He has been a surprisingly enthusiastic grandparent. He'd always seemed to be the more subdued of the couple, but he had taken to being a grandparent with zeal.

Ben's eyes fly open at the sound of his voice. "Pop!" He straightens and turns toward his pop, who then takes him from Rebecca.

I stand as Teddy approaches. He puts an arm around my shoulder and kisses my head. "How are you, sweetheart?"

Also unexpected, the bond I've formed with Teddy. I never had a dad until I met him. And Rebecca has turned into the mom I always wanted. I've not seen my birthmother in four years. And now, I have too much love in my life to care.

"I'm tired and hungry," I answer.

"You want your usual?" Rebecca asks. I nod, and she disappears to the kitchen.

"And how is Princess Parker?"

Yes, Alex and I named our baby girl for the Parkers. Ben is named after Alex's father, Benjamin, with the middle name Grant, which was Alex's Mom's last name before she got married.

"She only woke twice last night, so I'd say she's doing pretty good."

The restaurant suddenly goes quiet, and I don't have to look to know why. By and large, the town has gotten used to the mega movie star living amongst them, but for many, the novelty hasn't quite worn off. It certainly hasn't helped that press for his upcoming, and possibly last, movie is going strong.

"Ivy. What in the world? Do you know what it's like to wake up to an entirely empty house?"

I turn to face him fully.

"Good morning, my love," I say just as Ben throws his arms in the air and calls from his perch in Teddy's arms. "Daddy!"

And just like that, the frustration melts off his face. "Good morning, darlings." He leans down, wraps me and Parker in his arms, and kisses my cheek. Then he goes and takes Ben from his pop. "Good morning, Master Benjamin." Alex called Ben that once as a joke, and Ben thinks it's the absolute funniest thing. The joke continues.

Ben laughs and smashes his dad's cheeks in his hands.

"That's a good look for you." I laugh, then turn to Teddy. "Do you think you and Nana would be able to take a little break and join us for breakfast?"

He took a look around my restaurant and shrugged. "Maybe. Let me run and check in with Beck."

The Parkers moved to town right after they learned we were expecting Ben, our honeymoon baby. They'd fallen in love with the area on their first visit, and more so when they came back for our wedding. We had tossed around the idea of a destination wedding, but instead we opted for a small, intimate ceremony at our church, followed by a large and absolutely gorgeous party at a venue in town.

There wasn't anything keeping them in California, so they headed east and adopted us all—including Val and her family. My life was turning into more than I could have ever dreamed of, as the sad little girl whose only person in her life was her sister.

The Parkers also brought with them their restaurant experience and desire to keep working part-time. I'm on maternity leave now, but even when I'm not, they are in the restaurant at least twice a week.

"Am I your jailer, that you had to break out of the house?" Alex asks, pulling out a chair for me.

"I love you and I appreciate you, but your hovering and constant attention were about to make me lose my mind."

"I've been hovering, have I?"

"Yes."

"Was I hovering when I rubbed your neck last night?" He takes the seat beside me and puts his arm around my shoulder, settling Ben in his lap.

"Not at that moment."

"Was I hovering when I made dinner yesterday?"

"Alex." I laugh. "None of it's bad. It's just too much."

"I only want to take good care of you." He brings his hand from my shoulder to hold my head while he leans in to kiss my cheek.

"You do take care of me. You are the most loving and attentive husband. But sometimes I need a little space."

"I'm loving you too hard?"

I throw my head back and laugh. "Yes. Exactly, which shouldn't be much of a surprise given your personality and how hard you loved me *before* we had babies."

He sighs and smiles. "I'll try to tone it down. The three of you are just so lovable, it's hard to control."

I shake my head and smile at the man I call mine.

Val and her family show up and drag a table beside ours, just as Nana and Pop come out from the kitchen with four bowls. Tears fill my eyes as I stare around at my family.

"Are these good tears, darling?" Alex asks, pulling me toward him.

"The best tears."

Thank you for reading Alex & Ivy's story

Don't forget to leave a review or share with a friend!

Scan the QR code for a FREE BONUS EPILOGUE, or find

it on my website.

And continue reading for chapter one from

Sunshine & Cinnamon.

Sunshine & Cinnamon

Chapter 1: Chase

CHASE DAVIDSON SHIVERED IN disgust. His previous client, a woman in her early seventies, was making every effort to set Chase up with her "sexy" granddaughter. He certainly had nothing against said granddaughter; it was her grandmother's methods that made him squirm. Between the innuendo and blatant inappropriate comments, Chase had nearly ended the session early and asked her to leave. He was glad for a break between clients to clear his mind and refocus.

Chase had spent the past six-plus years living in Laurel Falls, a picturesque but largely undiscovered small town in Maine. Most of that time, he was fortunate enough to live in the apartment above The Sweet Spot Bakery, a little shop on Main Street with a vintage feel. The owner of the bakery, Amelia Butler, whom he called Ms. Millie, had become like a third grandmother to him. Her feistiness strongly reminded him of his gran. He helped her out as much as he could and she rewarded him with hugs and far too many sweet treats. They had a good relationship, which had made it extra confusing when she'd given him basically no notice that he had to move out because she needed the space.

Like most people, Chase hated to move. *But at least this way I won't be as likely to develop diabetes.* The thought led him to remember the old commercials with Wilford Brimley. *Dia-bee-tus.* Chase chuckled to himself. He had found a small house for rent on the edge of town at an incredible deal because the wealthy owner had a generous heart.

Since moving from his hometown in North Carolina, he had been working as a massage therapist at the Laurel Falls Spa, a full-service spa in a beautiful white Victorian house. He'd quickly become a favorite among the town's massage-needing clientele. He was also a favorite among the young women of the town, who were excited to have another male to choose from. He, however, never let them choose him. He had tried casual dating when he'd arrived in town, but he'd quickly realized that that wasn't the best idea living in such an isolated small town. Chase avoided all the sidelong glances, stepped back from all the touches, and redirected all the flirtatious conversations. Casual didn't work and he was leery of getting too close in a relationship. The possibility of loss seemed too great. The whole risk versus reward thing often didn't come out in reward's favor.

Chase was often found with world-renowned artist Ryan Kishlar, a man with whom he knew there was no possibility of getting too close. Mr. Kishlar had, in fact, been the greatest draw for his move to Laurel Falls. He was Chase's favorite painter, and as Chase had hoped, Mr. Kishlar had taken him under his wing. That is, if one considers having him clean the art studio and do landscaping as "under his wing." Mr. Kishlar did, however, let Chase observe him painting and offer words of wisdom on occasion, so Chase thought it was probably worth it to get to learn, even a bit, from a modern-day master.

During his break before his last client of the day, Chase sat at a table in the staff kitchen/break room. He sketched an idea he had for his next painting. *It's early morning and the rain from the night before has passed. What's left is dense fog that glows in the early-morning sunrise. Dark, contrasting shadows of tree trunks and rhododendron balance the warmth from the light, and the wet leaves make the colors more vibrant than usual. It's fall, but just barely, so green is still king. The other colors are beginning to make themselves known.*

Chase glanced at the clock, seeing it was two minutes until his last appointment for the day. He stood, stretching his arms and hands, then straightening his shirt. Had Chase known this would be the day his life changed, he would have worn his blue shirt. His mother always told him blue brought out his eyes. He never gave it much thought. Chase walked toward the living room that served as the waiting area for the spa. He spotted his client before she noticed him. He stopped in his tracks, momentarily forgetting how to breathe.

Standing near the sofa, in a stream of light from the window, was a woman whose hair looked as if it contained actual strands of gold. She looked beautifully pensive as she peered out the window. She wore dark high-waisted jean shorts and a top with a subtle floral pattern.

She was the most beautiful woman Chase had ever seen. *I can't believe I got massage oil in my hair during that last massage. What terrible timing. Although it might help to calm it down—it was a little unruly last I checked.* Chase continued to stare, frozen to his spot, his brain putting all of his energy into his eyes. *Her glasses are cuter on her than I thought glasses could be. Her hair looks so soft. And those legs.* He moved his eyes back up her body to her face. *She's a masterpiece.*

When Chase regained some of his faculties, he moved forward and spoke.

"Ruby? I'm ready for you."

The woman looked toward Chase.

"I'm glad you needed a massage today."

Realization dawning, Chase went wide-eyed. He schooled his features as quickly as he could. "I mean, I'm glad you're here. What brings you in for a massage today?"

He smiled his most professional smile and, heart hammering, awaited her response.

"You're *glad* I need a massage today?"

"No, of course not. I wouldn't want you to be in pain or overly stressed."

"That's nice, but then why would you say that?"

"I don't know. I massage a lot of old people and it was a pleasant surprise to see you. I mean, not pleasant, but different. It was different to see someone so beautiful come in. Not that I was thinking about you being beautiful and wanting to massage you. Your body's just different. Tight skin and all. Not that I was thinking about your tight skin. I actually noticed your hair first. I wasn't thinking about how nice it would be to massage you." *Stop talking, you idiot.*

She stared at him, her face a mixture of shock and anger covered by a thin veil of politeness. "I feel like that was exactly what you were thinking."

"It wasn't." *Not exactly.*

She continued to stare at him, seeming to consider her next words or move.

This isn't going to be good.

"This is unbelievable and absolutely unprofessional. You should not be in this line of work if you can't do better than this. Where is the manager?"

Am I about to throw up in front of this woman? How can I fix this?

"I am so sorry. I don't know what came over me. This isn't who I am. The owner isn't here right now, but I'm begging you not to contact her. I really need this job. How about a massage with Janie? On me. She's a very talented massage therapist. She doesn't have any more appointments today, but she owes me a favor. I could make it happen very soon, I'm sure."

"For some reason, I'm feeling a little weird about getting massages right now. I can't believe this—I had heard such great things about this place and *you* in particular. And my back is so tight, so you'll understand if I am more than a little ticked."

"I do. I really do. I can't apologize enough. If you would be comfortable with it, I could work on your back just standing here out in the open. Just until it loosens enough for you to have some relief." *Idiot. Idiot. Idiot.*

Ruby eyed him, considering. She looked toward the window, pushing her glasses up her nose. "You're not going to do anything stupid, are you?" she asked, looking back his way, a stern but rather cute look on her face.

"No. Absolutely not. And there are three ladies cutting hair in the next room, so you could always yell. Although, I promise there will be no need." *Oh my gosh, I've messed up. Please forgive me and let's move on and forget this ever happened. Why does she have to be so cute in her glasses? I wonder if she's a nerd.*

I'd love that. Stop it, Chase!

"Yes, okay. I guess I'm desperate, so let's do that. Just know, I will not hesitate to scream," Ruby said with that stern/cute look.

"Noted. Come over here, closer to the hair salon." She moved toward him. "Let me run and grab a ponytail holder to keep your hair out of the way."

Chase took the opportunity during his short journey to the salon to take a few deep steadying breaths and gather himself. *I can do this. I can massage this girl professionally and make her realize that I'm not an awful person who deserves to lose his job. I'm good at what I do and that's why I do it. I'm certainly not a pervert. I can't help it if she's so pretty that my brain stopped working, can I? Stupid brain, get your act together.*

Walking back into the room, he decided it might be a good start to introduce himself. "I'm Chase, by the way. You know, in case you need a name for your voodoo doll."

Ruby scoffed, but he could have sworn he saw the corner of her mouth twitch. She pulled up her hair and he stepped behind her, noting the difference in their heights. *It seems like she's about six or seven inches shorter than me. So that puts her at five seven or eight. Why does that matter, Chase? Focus!* "I'm going to start if you're still okay with it."

"Yes. Go ahead," Ruby said, taking in and releasing a deep breath.

Wow. She really does need a massage and I ruined it for her like a big jerk. I'll give her the best awkward standing massage I can and fix this. Chase took another deep breath. *Mistake. She smells like sunshine and cookies. Okay. Hands on autopilot, brain on something distracting. Tomorrow's to-do list. Buy groceries. Finish unpacking. Well, that certainly sounds like an exciting day off. Maybe Mr. Kishlar will let me come over for a while. Ruby is such a nice name. I should incorporate some ruby into my painting. I'd like to paint her. Look at all the color variations in her hair. I'd have a hard time capturing that, but I'd like to try. I missed her eye color, I'll have to... stop it, Chase! Good grief. Okay, other things. Maybe I should try to plant a garden this...*

"Yes. Right there seems to be the worst of it," Ruby said, startling him out of his thoughts.

"Ah. Yeah, it does feel like it could be the source of your problems. You obviously needed this, I'm so sorry." Chase paused and, when she didn't respond, continued, "What have you been up to that has you messed up?"

"The phrase 'lift with your legs' didn't occur to me until it was too late."

"That will do it. Some heat followed by stretching should help. Maybe some ice before bed tonight. But like I said, I'll get you in with Janie soon. Your contact info is already in the system. She'll give you a call."

Chase continued working in her problem area and he could feel her relaxing under his touch. Suddenly a moan started to slip out of her mouth, but she caught herself and stepped away from Chase.

Ruby had seemed to realize she had relaxed rather too much to maintain her attitude of righteous indignation toward him. She stiffened her posture and pursed her lips. Without thinking, Chase said, "You're going to ruin what we just did."

Ruby looked at him like he was an idiot and left, slamming the door behind her.

Her eyes are like moss just after a good rain.

Thank you for reading the first chapter of Sunshine & Cinnamon! You can find it, along with the rest of the Laurel Falls series, on Amazon.

Also by the Author

The Laurel Falls Series

Sunshine & Cinnamon

Love & Shooting Stars

Flurries & First Love

Blossoms & Breezes

The Love on Vacation Series

Let's Pretend

Book 2 coming 2026

Letters to Mrs. Claus Multi-Author Series

Cozy by the Fire(man)

Please leave a review on Amazon and/or Goodreads. It's the most important thing you can do for an indie author. Thanks in advance!!!

Head to LindsayRochester.com to read *A New Adventure* for free!

Or scan here:

ACKNOWLEDGEMENTS

First, I want to thank God for the strength and energy to do all the things that go into writing and releasing not only this book, but Cozy by the Fire(man), as well. I couldn't have done it, and all the life things, without Him.

Tiffany, where have you been all my life? LOL. I'm so happy to have found you. Your friendship and the bookish camaraderie we have mean the world to me. I'm so looking forward to all our writing adventures! Also, I promise you had funny comments! :)

Maylan, I know I already told you this, but getting your late-night comments when I woke in the morning felt like Christmas. Your feedback is a treasure I'd be lost without. Also, I think everyone who isn't your cousin should be jealous.

Lacey, thank you especially for helping me get the migraine

scene right. You know how I want things to be as accurate as possible. One of my favorite memories is talking with you about Sunshine & Cinnamon in Mom's living room. It floored me how much you liked it, and I'm grateful you've been on my team ever since!

Natalie, I'm so glad we got to have an actual "mum" in this book! It was such a comfort to know you would not let me screw up any of the English things! It was a pleasure working with you, as always.

Melody, this cover ... Sheeh, you know what you're doing! I'm so grateful to you for creating what is really a dream cover. Thank you.

D, I'm so grateful for your support. I couldn't do this without you. There aren't words to say how much I love you; just know that ours is my favorite love story.